# Playtime Poets
Edited by Mark Richardson

First published in Great Britain in 2008 by:
Young Writers
Remus House
Coltsfoot Drive
Peterborough
PE2 9JX
Telephone: 01733 890066
Website: www.youngwriters.co.uk

All Rights Reserved

© *Copyright Contributors 2008*

SB ISBN 978-1 84431 695 3

# Foreword

Young Writers was established in 1991 and has been passionately devoted to the promotion of reading and writing in children and young adults ever since. The quest continues today. Young Writers remains as committed to the nurturing of poetic and literary talent as ever.

This year's Young Writers competition has proven as vibrant and dynamic as ever and we are delighted to present a showcase of the best poetry from across the UK and in some cases overseas. Each poem has been selected from a wealth of *Little Laureates 2008* entries before ultimately being published in this, our seventeenth primary school poetry series.

Once again, we have been supremely impressed by the overall quality of the entries we have received. The imagination, energy and creativity which has gone into each young writer's entry made choosing the poems a challenging and often difficult but ultimately hugely rewarding task - the general high standard of the work submitted ensured this opportunity to bring their poetry to a larger appreciative audience.

We sincerely hope you are pleased with this final collection and that you will enjoy *Little Laureates 2008 Playtime Poets* for many years to come.

# Contents

| | |
|---|---|
| Emma Bannister (9) | 1 |
| Ebony Freer (10) | 1 |
| Victoria Smith (9) | 2 |
| Codie Nolan (9) | 2 |
| Evan Jewers (11) | 3 |
| Saffiya Tariq (8) | 4 |
| Sophie England (10) | 4 |
| Joel Maxwell-Thompson (10) | 4 |
| Neive Wilde (9) | 5 |
| Brad Watts (9) | 5 |
| Calum McDonald (7) | 5 |
| Hesham Hegazy (10) | 6 |
| Rhaeila Begum & Sarah Pareen (10) | 6 |
| Ellis Wakelin (10) | 7 |
| Luca Huber-Nagy (11) | 7 |
| Heather Thomas (10) | 8 |
| William Bond (8) | 8 |
| Lucy Smith (10) | 9 |
| Emma Ward (9) | 9 |
| Matthew Andrew (10) | 10 |
| Cathrene Mieras (10) | 10 |
| Lewis Pryce-Jones (11) | 10 |
| Raisa Hegazy (11) | 11 |
| Laura Ward (10) | 11 |

### XII Apostle's RC Primary School, Leigh

| | |
|---|---|
| Callam Garvey (10) | 12 |
| Megan Worthington (11) | 12 |
| Ross Greenhalgh (10) | 12 |
| Danielle Atherton (11) | 13 |
| Jennifer Shovelton (11) | 13 |
| Sean Smith (11) | 13 |
| Sepultura Tranter (11) | 14 |
| Catherine Clews (10) | 14 |
| Oliver Wilcock (10) | 14 |
| Adam Ashurst (11) | 15 |
| Sam Purslow (11) | 15 |
| Florence Wu (10) | 15 |
| Thomas Fallon (11) | 16 |

| | |
|---|---|
| Jasmin Faulkner (11) | 16 |
| Jack Morris (10) | 16 |
| Jessica Sephton (11) | 17 |
| Hannah Ratcliffe (11) | 17 |
| Elisha Hayes (10) | 17 |

**Barley Hill Primary School, Thame**

| | |
|---|---|
| Taylor Shurrock (9) | 18 |
| Sam Shannon (9) | 19 |
| Megan Carter (9) | 20 |
| Charlotte Norton (10) | 21 |
| Hester Cameron (7) | 22 |
| Zoe Chatterton (7) | 22 |
| Vicky Kingston (11) | 23 |
| Imogene Alice Goodman (9) | 23 |
| Joely Brewer (7) | 24 |
| Isobel Glover (7) | 24 |
| Annabel Britton (8) | 25 |
| Eleanor Shearwood (10) | 25 |
| Casey Stanley (9) | 26 |
| Hayden Brewer (6) | 26 |
| Samuel Pickup (8) | 26 |
| Cosette Jackson (10) | 27 |
| Gunishi Nathoo (9) | 27 |
| Isobel Scarborough (8) | 27 |

**Beechwood School, Guernsey**

| | |
|---|---|
| Toby Glass (8) | 28 |
| Jamie Hall (7) | 28 |
| Brent Oldfield (7) | 29 |
| Nairn Guilbert (8) | 29 |
| David Millar (8) | 30 |
| Don Harty (7) | 30 |
| Daniel Davies (9) | 31 |
| Rory Johnson (7) | 31 |
| Joshua Shand (9) | 32 |
| Sammy Fowler (8) | 32 |
| Teddy Gordon Le-Clerc (8) | 33 |
| Anthony Stokes (9) | 33 |
| Jools Houston (9) | 34 |
| Joseph Gillson (8) | 34 |

| | |
|---|---|
| George Orton (9) | 35 |
| Bradley Norman (9) | 35 |
| Alexander King (9) | 36 |
| Oliver Le Marquand (9) | 36 |
| Elliott Cockett (9) | 37 |
| Bertie Charman (11) | 37 |
| Finley Spence (8) | 38 |
| Jacob Trott (9) | 38 |

**Birralee International School Trondheim, Trondheim, Norway**

| | |
|---|---|
| Conrad Bali & Mats Langseth (10) | 39 |
| Ludger Albert Moser (10) | 39 |
| Naol Saba (9) | 40 |
| Rebecca Gjaevran Saether (10) | 40 |
| Natasha Zotcheva (9) | 40 |
| Vanessa Alstad (9) | 41 |
| Hedda Nødtvedt (11) | 41 |
| Marius Haugstad (9) | 41 |
| Camilla Steen (10) | 42 |
| Martine Brun (11) | 42 |
| Adrian Langseth (9) | 42 |

**Blakesley CE Primary School, Towcester**

| | |
|---|---|
| Laura Pratley (11) | 43 |
| Katie Noble (11) | 44 |
| Simon Walker (11) | 44 |
| Aidan Louw (10) | 45 |
| Louise Duffy (10) | 45 |
| Vincenzo Pratley (10) | 46 |
| Natalya Zajko (10) | 47 |
| Abbey-Anne Gyles (10) | 48 |

**Castel Primary School, Guernsey**

| | |
|---|---|
| Rebecca Cox (9) | 48 |
| Ewan Edward Reynolds (9) | 49 |
| Sophie Le Feuvre (8) | 49 |
| Lota Nwokolo (10) | 50 |
| Katie Anderson (10) | 50 |
| Robyn Munro (8) | 51 |
| Bernice Saunders (7) | 51 |
| Kirsty Standring (9) | 52 |

## Edward Field CP School, Kidlington

| | |
|---|---|
| Skye Turner  (11) | 52 |
| Edward Hopkin  (10) | 52 |
| Kieran Kilcoyne  (8) | 53 |
| Emily Hurdley  (11) | 53 |
| Martha Cook  (10) | 54 |
| Genevieve Tomes  (10) | 55 |
| Darryl Salmon  (10) | 56 |
| Toby Cole  (10) | 56 |
| Rachel Barrett  (11) | 57 |
| Kamran Afzal  (10) | 57 |
| Phoebe Knight  (10) | 58 |
| Danielle Hollis  (11) | 58 |
| Jade Ghanbary  (10) | 59 |
| Magnus Taylor  (10) | 59 |
| Robbie Jacques  (11) | 60 |

## Flore CE Primary School, Northampton

| | |
|---|---|
| Joshua Goddard  (9) | 60 |
| Lorna Butler  (10) | 61 |
| Karampreet Kaur  (10) | 61 |
| Joanna Bucknall  (9) | 62 |
| Haydn Groves  (9) | 62 |
| Molly Smith  (10) | 62 |
| Gemma Jones  (11) | 63 |
| Jack Walton  (10) | 63 |
| Jacob Ogden  (9) | 63 |
| Charley Rideout  (10) | 64 |
| Emily Cousins  (10) | 64 |
| Ben Kingston  (10) | 65 |
| Ellie Cockerill  (9) | 65 |
| Jemma Mason  (11) | 66 |
| Reuben Lownes  (9) | 66 |
| Alex Bucknall  (11) | 66 |
| Bryony Mead  (10) | 67 |
| George Underwood  (11) | 67 |
| Amy Welbourne  (11) | 67 |
| Alexander Morehen  (10) | 68 |
| Elliot Wilde  (10) | 68 |
| Jake Howard  (11) | 68 |
| Abigail Wright  (10) | 69 |

Sam Norman  (10)     69
Alex Salmons  (9)     69

**Gilberdyke Primary School, Brough**
Yasin Tall  (10)     70
Angus Harvey  (9)     70
Shannon Rastrick  (9)     70
Katie Last  (9)     71
Amy Woodward  (9)     71
Danielle Hardgrave  (10)     71
Tom Shanks  (10)     72
Joe Huntley  (9)     72
Megan Malcolmson  (10)     73
Joseph Allen  (10)     73
Joe Sefton  (10)     73
Molly Brown  (10)     74

**Harwell Primary School, Didcot**
Alex Downes  (10)     74
James Hartley  (11)     75
Anna Hobin  (10)     75
Charlotte Adams  (10)     76
Rosie Fishburn  (9)     76
Elinor Clarke  (11)     77
Joshua Samuel Buttery  (9)     77
Charlotte Grocutt  (10)     78
Gemma Tankard  (9)     78
Annie Vickers  (9)     78
Jessica Brady  (10)     79
Jack Constant  (10)     79
Laura Passau  (10)     80
Robert Dickens  (11)     81
Eleanor Turner  (11)     82

**Leighfield Primary School, Uppingham**
Theo Jones  (9)     82
Sophie Wilks  (11)     83
George Gutteridge  (8)     83
Bethany Turiccki  (11)     84
Elliott Bentley  (11)     84

| | |
|---|---:|
| Lauren Rootham (11) | 85 |
| Daniel Pallett (10) | 85 |
| Adam MacDonald (11) | 86 |
| Harry Martin (11) | 87 |
| Calypso Keightley (11) | 88 |
| Charlotte Gregg (10) | 89 |
| Molly King (10) | 90 |
| Josh Christian (9) | 90 |
| Iona Collins (10) | 91 |
| Jennifer Hemmings (10) | 91 |
| Gregory Sale (11) | 92 |
| Beatrix Wignall (11) | 93 |
| Megan Wright (10) | 94 |
| Rosie Mottershead (9) | 94 |
| Charley Munro Scott (10) | 95 |
| Sabrina Lucas (10) | 95 |
| Harry Wade (10) | 96 |
| Daniel Webster (11) | 97 |
| Louisa Newell (11) | 98 |
| Rebecca Sale (8) | 99 |
| Angela Wilson (8) | 100 |
| Thomas Little (8) | 100 |
| Alex Brookes (9) | 100 |
| Phoebe Lawton (9) | 101 |
| Fay Wilkins (9) | 101 |
| Lucy Wade (8) | 101 |
| James Aleixo (9) | 102 |
| Alex MacDonald | 102 |
| Luke Griffiths | 102 |
| Connor Griggs (9) | 103 |
| Harry Stuart (8) | 103 |
| George Newcomb-Harvey (9) | 103 |
| Thomas Beach (9) | 104 |
| Josh Foley (9) | 104 |
| Jamie Duggan (9) | 104 |
| Lacey Holbrook (8) | 105 |
| Thea Crutchley (8) | 105 |

# The Poems

## Horse Riding

Horses brushed and tacked up ready,
Off we trot, nice and steady,
Through the gate and up the hill,
By the stream and trees so still.

Clipperty-clop, the sound of hooves,
Trotting along she freely moves,
We have a canter and jump a log,
Taking care in the gloomy fog.

The horse heads back as fast as she's able,
A bucket awaiting in the stable,
Her hay net filled and smelling sweet,
She can finally rest her aching feet.

**Emma Bannister (9)**


## The Mirror

She stares at you and copies
any face you pull

She helps you by sitting
patiently on the wall

Judging whatever you do
with her smooth brown body

She thinks, *what is the next person
going to look like?*

*What am I going to look like?*

Well she might as well smile
because it's over.

**Ebony Freer (10)**

## Think Green

Recycle to stop global warming,
Re-use to stop garbage forming,
The charity shop may accept what you take,
There are loads of great things you can make,
Take your bottles to the bottle bank,
When all the liquid has been drank,
Put all your veg skins on the compost heap,
To make the flowers grow tall and the roots grow deep,
If you have a recycling bin,
You can put your paper in,
Why not walk rather than go in your car,
If you are not going far,
When you're done, turn the lights out,
You will be saving energy no doubt,
Make sure your tap has no drops,
To make sure that the water has stopped.

**Victoria Smith (9)**


## Night Sky

In the night sky clouds force through the wind,
The stars flash like diamonds trying to catch your eye.

Wolves singing to praise the spirits,
Angels come together and dance in the wind.

Feeling the breeze blowing in your face,
Calms you down from stressing about things.

The sky takes spirits across the sky,
People say your grandad and nana are up in Heaven.

**Codie Nolan (9)**

## At Old Portsmouth

At Old Portsmouth,
I hear the powerful sea thrashing
And slapping against the boats.
I see the yachts bobbing around,
Within the harbour.
I hear the seagulls screaming with loneliness,
Their sound makes me want to cry,
I hear children chattering with excitement and laughter.

At Old Portsmouth,
I see gulls guarding the naked sky,
A single lonely cloud gliding over the Spinnaker Tower,
I see a mini tornado of leaves round my feet,
And clouds gathering and towering about me,
I see the lights of Portsmouth go out
And a flash of lightning hitting the ground.

At Old Portsmouth,
I smell the smoke from a nearby factory,
I smell rotting fish,
Like eggs left untouched for years,
I smell the salty sea,
And the delightful smell,
Of fresh fish and chips,
As I pass the shop.

I feel the wind pushing against me,
And friends tapping me on the shoulder,
Telling me to hurry up.

**Evan Jewers (11)**

## Terms

There are 4 terms, like summer,
Summer is a very hot term,
So watch out for the sun,
And keep yourself cool,
It is one of the best terms,
Not like winter,
Winter is a very cold term,
So I'll say keep yourself warm.
Spring is when the flowers start to gleam
And it's when you can have a party and have some fun,
Autumn is when you get colder.

**Saffiya Tariq (8)**


## Shark

Silent but deadly, she is the enemy of the ocean,
Her mouth is as big as the ocean, she attacks like
A jaguar pouncing onto their prey,
She is graceful as she moves in the gloom,
She is smoke-blue with a hint of electric-blue,
She is silent as she moves in the ocean,
She has one enemy, human kind.

**Sophie England (10)**


## The Rugby Game!

R elish in the atmosphere,
U mpteenth tackle, ow that hurt,
G lory for the winning side,
B rilliant game lads,
Y ou're definitely coming back!

**Joel Maxwell-Thompson (10)**

## Next Door's Cat

Next door's cat is a horrible thing,
It miaows while I'm trying to sing,
It climbs on the shed and eats the bird's bread instead.
It ate my friend's fish and
Broke my mum's favourite dish and ran away with
                               the fish in its tummy,
It scratched my poor mummy and fell on its tummy
And chased a rat until it was flat,
Poor little rat, all dead and flat.

What a stupid cat!

**Neive Wilde (9)**


## Santa's Poem

See Santa at night,
He will have a fright,
So make sure that you're tucked up tight,
Santa's sleigh with the bells on the right,
Give him a fright in the light,
Give him a jumper to keep him warm,
Give him a light, so he can see the way.

**Brad Watts (9)**


## Snowflakes

Snowflakes,
Flying, spinning, tumbling,
Shining and magical,
Hides the mountains,
Cold and soft,
Snowflakes.

**Calum McDonald (7)**

## The Rainbow Poem

After raining for three hours,
I went out for sugar and flowers,
Through drizzle and light showers,
A rainbow showed with pretty colours,
'Its promising wealth and powers,'
Said Dad, wishing it all were ours.

A giant half circle in the sky,
Touching the home of a lucky guy,
'Get the treasure,' I heard Daddy's sigh,
'Let's follow the rainbow or let's fly.'
We got there and did the work of a spy,
Looking everywhere, low and high,
We found nothing but a cat with one eye,
The cat said, 'No treasure, you know why?
The rainbow is gone and weather is dry.'

**Hesham Hegazy (10)**


## Love

Love is happiness for my family,
Love smells like candyfloss,
Love looks like laughter,
Love is a beautiful feeling,
For example, relaxing on the sofa,
Love is the colour of the sky,
It's fresh blue,
It tastes like a Valentine heart

**Rhaeila Begum & Sarah Pareen (10)**

## Animals!

Animals are everywhere,
Monkey, giraffe and even bear!
I like them all, big and small,
Or maybe even short and tall!

Wild animals aren't that scary,
But some of them are really hairy!
Some noisy and some quiet,
Perhaps they have a healthy diet!

Most pets are really great,
But some people really hate,
Snakes, mice, dogs and cats,
But I like them all, even rats!

**Ellis Wakelin (10)**

## Cry Of The Helpless

I am crying next to the Moon, in the dark,
My head is full of darkness,
I do not know what to write.

My ideas are flashing in,
My head, like some light
In the darkness, lights up
Some sparks.

I have my idea to write,
So I have written this poem,
For those who are in the dark.

**Luca Huber-Nagy (11)**

## The River's Story

I remember when life was good,
I enjoyed those days,
I saw sheep giving birth,
Fawns tumbling, trying to stand,
I sparkled in the night,
Like a hundred fallen stars.

Ducklings swam joyfully,
Lilies like crows, grew on my head,
Water boatmen rowed on my skin,
I was happy, as happy as could be.

Factories shrunk my glory,
I am old now, nearly dead,
I cannot live forever,
I am just a shadow,
A shadow of Man's way.

Now I wear garbage as a dunce hat,
I am green and swollen,
I am not noticed,
Silent and dead for Hell bears the way.

**Heather Thomas (10)**


## The Writer Of This Poem
*(Inspired by 'The Writer of this Poem' by Roger McGough)*

Is as strong as a wall,
Is as light as a feather,
Is as fast as a cheetah,
Is as sly as a fox,
Is as good at football as Wayne Rooney,
Is as silly as a clown,
Is as bright as the sun,
And as happy as a monkey.

**William Bond (8)**

## My Magic Box
*(Based on 'Magic Box' by Kit Wright)*

I will put in my box . . .

The snap of the climbing tree branches,
The smooth pink silk in the clothes shop,
Two thin fingers braiding a strand of hair.

I will put in my box . . .

The swish of the ice skates rubbing on the ice,
The taste of saltwater from the Mediterranean Sea,
The Maori of New Zealand performing their dance.

I will put in my box . . .

Baby Murray's cheery smile,
My granny Adams' gentle voice,
All my family from abroad, living in Scotland.

I will put in my box . . .

A year full of summers,
Spies shopping for designer clothes,
Ashley Tisdale hiding and sneaking.

My box is made from,
Silk and pink ribbon,
My lid is made from gleaming lilac diamonds,
My hinges are bluebird wings.

I shall flip over the Eiffel Tower and land on my feet in Paris,
Then I will lie myself down in the streets of Wellington
Amongst the pinkest flowers.

**Lucy Smith (10)**


## Sun - Haiku

It shines down on us
Beaming all day children smile
Shining through the sky.

**Emma Ward (9)**

## Colour Poem

Light blue is the sky,
Light blue is the ocean on a warm day,
Light blue is a cold day,
Light blue tastes like a blueberry ice lollipop,
Light blue smells like an air freshener,
Light blue sounds like a CD,
Light blue feels like snow,
Light blue looks like the sky,
Light blue makes other people sad,
Light blue is my favourite colour.

**Matthew Andrew (10)**

## The Storm

The lightning struck across the sky.
The leaves on the trees flew extremely high.
The rain came down in lashing torrents.
And the wind was such a horror.
There was a deafening crash. It was the thunder's almighty blast.
Hail was falling like a bullet from a gun.
An inky black sky covered the glowing sun.
A powerful tornado,
Hovered over the Earth,
Hoovering up everything in its path.

**Cathrene Mieras (10)**

## Art

Art is using imagination and our soul's freedom,
To create objects, pictures and feelings,
Doing, creating, making and standing out from others,
This is all art.

**Lewis Pryce-Jones (11)**

## My Dream

I was sleeping on a cloud and floating in the sky,
I could feel all the white feathers swirling from a white bird to my toes,
Sleeping on a cloud and taking me to see the world,
Just like an explorer, (what I've always wanted to be).
Just then I woke up, I could see a rainbow above me,
I skipped from cloud to cloud to get to the rainbow,
I went to each colour one by one,
*It was amazing!*
Then I flew on top of the rainbow to get to the pot of gold,
When I got there, the gold was shining directly at my eyes,
Just as if I was staring at the sun for an hour!
Suddenly I didn't know where I was going and
                        I fell miles down from the sky,
Until I found myself in the water,
I didn't want my dream to end,
So I swam to a dolphin and then he took me to meet all the fishes,
They were singing to me at first,
It was just like the story of the Little Mermaid,
Then the dolphin came back to me and threw me back
                        up to the sky on my cloud,
Then I went back to sleep,
Too bad, I ended my dream when I didn't want to.

**Raisa Hegazy (11)**


## My Dad

My dad is a deep blue,
He is autumn,
In a cool swimming pool,
And warm blue skies,
He is a blue T-shirt,
And a warm comfy bed,
He is a nature programme,
And yummy scones with cream on top.

**Laura Ward (10)**

## The Elephant

The elephant is marching like a soldier guarding a castle,
Ripping bark off the trees,
Then slurps up nearly all the lake,
The elephant is running as fast as a cheetah
To get away from the hungry lion,
He throws the lion with his strong trunk,
Some juicy fruit, he goes getting.

**Callam Garvey (10)**
XII Apostle's RC Primary School, Leigh

## The Delicate Dolphin

In the deep blue distance,
She shimmers in the ocean,
Playing and diving with her beloved parents,
In the sunset, watch them dancing away,
Happily and joyfully,
See them gliding underwater and ten leaping into the air,
Feel her soft, smooth and shiny skin
Bouncing off the sun and lighting up the sky,
Listen to the ocean flowing and splashing,
As they make their way home.

**Megan Worthington (11)**
XII Apostle's RC Primary School, Leigh

## Penguins

His chest bursting like a rich proud king,
Diving in the sea like an Olympic diver,
Snapping his beak like a crocodile,
Flapping his wings faster than an F1 driver.

His wings as smooth as a pebble,
His white chest camouflaging in the snow,
And the little fellow is smaller than a wall,
And his little feet can only take him so slow.

**Ross Greenhalgh (10)**
XII Apostle's RC Primary School, Leigh

# Penguin

The eager penguin waddles through its home of freezing ice,
Watching its baby as if it were a spy,
Struggling through the icy knives which grow around her,
As her baby pushes onwards, she watches him fall and slide around
On the rock-hard sea of ice.

**Danielle Atherton (11)**
XII Apostle's RC Primary School, Leigh

# The Penguin

It waddles in the icy cold air,
Its soft feathers protecting it from the cold like
A mother wrapping her baby up so it's warm,
He keeps tripping as he toddles for miles and miles,
Like an unsteady toddler who has just learnt to walk,
His webbed feet are moving,
Closer and closer it gets,
Then suddenly it leaps like an antelope running
And gets swallowed up by the colossal sharp sea.

**Jennifer Shovelton (11)**
XII Apostle's RC Primary School, Leigh

# Elephant

Out in the savannah, a huge elephant,
Like a swordsman swings its trunk,
The smell is awful,
It's just like a skunk.

He sways his tail like a skipping rope
To see off the flies,
They roam around the jungle,
Acting like spies.

**Sean Smith (11)**
XII Apostle's RC Primary School, Leigh

## Baby Cub

The baby cub bent around curves quickly
And suddenly, like a car turning,
She got ready to pounce and carefully stepped back slowly,
Then lying down under the sea, her fur coat shining bright,
Her big ears twitching like a kangaroo hopping very happily,
Her tail shimmering when she swooped it in the sharp wind,
A shine gleaming from her pearly eyes
Like a person smiling from far away.

**Sepultura Tranter (11)**
XII Apostle's RC Primary School, Leigh


## Dolphin

With quick moves she jumps into the water,
As the blazing sun heats her up,
People cheer as she performs her outstanding tricks,
Swaying her tail under the hot sun,
Her skin so smooth it glistens in the water,
Splashing her tail like an angry adult stomping around.

On the surface of the water,
In the crystal-clear water,
Her mouth sings with happiness.

**Catherine Clews (10)**
XII Apostle's RC Primary School, Leigh


## Dolphin

Smooth and elegant through the sea,
Every time it comes out showing it's fins and squeals,
The skin as grey as a cloud,
The noise he makes aloud,
And when you think it is complete,
He dives back into the crystal-blue water.

**Oliver Wilcock (10)**
XII Apostle's RC Primary School, Leigh

## Gorilla

The gorilla leaping from its green bristly tree looking for food,
Always looking after its babies.

Like a rugby player gripping the gorilla's family,
Gripping to a tree,
The tropical rainforest below them.

Found some bananas at last,
So the family can eat.

**Adam Ashurst (11)**
XII Apostle's RC Primary School, Leigh

## Elegant Eagle

Like a parrot at the zoo, he sits perched on a branch,
Waiting for some food like a lion searching for its prey,
Like crystals in the blazing sun his eyes gleam,
Sharply he spots his prey and starts to circle it,
Like a pilot landing a plane, he swoops down and
Grabs the mouse with his feet,
His catch puts up a fight but
Like a wrestler, it submits,
Like a baby going to sleep, it breathes its last.

**Sam Purslow (11)**
XII Apostle's RC Primary School, Leigh

## Dolphin

Swimming fins smoothly glide,
The dolphin is full of pride,
It does a somersault, showing off,
Thinking as light as a cloth,
His spraying hole is like a water gun,
He is the only one,
He's the best . . .
Well, better than all the rest!

**Florence Wu (10)**
XII Apostle's RC Primary School, Leigh

## The Dazzling Dolphin

Like a bullet out a gun, the dazzling dolphin leaps into mid-air,
With its streamlined body, it dives into the early morning sea,
Speeding to the bottom of the sea to find his prey,
So quiet, so quiet, then . . . *crunch!*
He has captured his prey,
Between his teeth the fish struggles
To get away. . . . But there's no hope now,
The dolphin slowly rests and
Gracefully snores . . . *sshh, sshh, sshh.*

**Thomas Fallon (11)**
XII Apostle's RC Primary School, Leigh


## Monkey

The jolly cheeky monkey,
Climbing a large tree,
Like a fireman saving a kitten,
The monkey being so greedy,
Looks for some fresh bananas,
Like an inspector being picky,
The monkey seeing a banana
Eats it and runs.

**Jasmin Faulkner (11)**
XII Apostle's RC Primary School, Leigh


## The Dolphin

The dolphin plays blissfully,
He jumps! He dives!
A fish dives down like a lion catching his prey,
The fish moves rapidly,
The dolphin briskly dives,
He's caught his prey.

**Jack Morris (10)**
XII Apostle's RC Primary School, Leigh

## Lion Cub

Lying in the soundless grass,
The lion cub is as quiet as a peaceful ballerina dancing in the night,
The lion grabs the prey and is as clingy as a monkey to a tree.

**Jessica Sephton (11)**
XII Apostle's RC Primary School, Leigh


## Elephant

As hot as the sun the elephant lay, tired,
Its humungous eyes fixed on the ice-cold water,
It got up weary, however, it still attempted to run to the water,
Eventually it got there, flooded with sweat,
Like a hose, its trunk splashes itself with water.

**Hannah Ratcliffe (11)**
XII Apostle's RC Primary School, Leigh


## The Lion Cub

The dry grassy field hides and protects it,
The lion spots the prey,
Like an eagle spotting a minute mouse,
It prowls silently,
Like a child playing hide-and-seek,
Then it pounces.

It leaps into the warm summery air,
And catches the animal,
Between its razor-sharp teeth,
Causing it to struggle and panic,
The lion doesn't care about the prey,
Just about its full stomach.

**Elisha Hayes (10)**
XII Apostle's RC Primary School, Leigh

## Can You Guess?

Can you guess what sport I am?
If you can you're as wise as an owl,
This sport you play on a bench,
Are you puzzled?
I am,
You play it in a sport,
Confused?

You can play it in shorts, T-shirt, or even a skirt,
In training you run about,
But in a match, you're frozen solid,
Like an ice cube,
Have you guessed yet?

No!

Well here we go!
It can only add up to one thing,
Well, it's not a sport really.
Well I'll tell you!

It's a . . . sub!
On the bench with your manager,
So there we go - a sub you know.

**Taylor Shurrock (9)**
**Barley Hill Primary School, Thame**

## The Laptop

Once I logged onto my PC,
My sister was about to scream!
I went onto the Internet,
And searched for groceries,
I clicked on the first link,
The top link,
The best of them all,
Then . . .
There was an advertisement,
It said I was a winner!
A winner of what?
A winner of a laptop!
Apparently I was the 1,000th visitor,
I was overjoyed,
I typed in my details,
Unfortunately . . .
I had to be over 14,
I was only 10,
I typed my age as 15,
And clicked submit . . .
Three days later there was a knock at the door!
They asked to see me,
So I came to the door,
I was in *big trouble!*

**Sam Shannon (9)**
**Barley Hill Primary School, Thame**

## School

Five hundred children,
Walk into the hall,
Waiting in assembly,
Waiting for the Head to speak to all.

Some of them are young,
Some of them are old,
Some of them have hair,
1 or 2 are bald.

The Head is talking,
A real lot,
Some children are listening,
Some are not,
Now it is over, we go back to class.

It is maths now,
We do lots of addition,
A little division,
Some subtraction.

Some sums are hard,
Others are easy,
Some children are bored,
A few are quite happy,
It is break - hooray!

We act like monkeys,
Kicking a ball,
Playing with friends, the fun never ends,
The naughty children sit in the hall.

**Megan Carter (9)**
**Barley Hill Primary School, Thame**

## How I'd Like To Move?

I like to run and skip all day,
I like to jump and hop along the way,
I like to dance, I like to move,
I like to just boogie and groove.

I'd like to bounce like a bunny rabbit,
But people would think it's a funny habit,
I'd like to run like a cheetah, ever so fast,
So when I'm in a race, I'd never come last.

I'd like to slither like a slippery snake,
Or just float like a swan on a lake,
I'd like to fly like a bird up high,
Or soar like a plane in the sky.

I'd like to prowl like a great big cat,
Or hang upside down just like a bat,
I'd like to swim like a scaly fish,
There are so many things I could wish.

I'd like to swing just like a monkey,
Then my friends would think I'm so funky,
I'd like to fly and buzz like a bee,
But really I'm just happy being me.

I like to run and skip all day,
I like to jump and hop along the way,
I like to dance, I like to move,
I like to just boogie and groove.

**Charlotte Norton (10)**
**Barley Hill Primary School, Thame**

## Movement Poem

I like to move all around,
In the air and on the ground,
I love to travel on a train,
And enjoy flying on a plane.
I always look out at night,
When the stars are shining bright,
And see the wind moving the trees,
And hear the lovely gentle breeze.
When I go to the beach I see the waves crash on the sand,
As I swim in my rubber band,
I also learnt something I didn't know,
It's that the Earth spins not at all slow,
And at the end of the day I go to bed,
And have to rest my sleepy head.

**Hester Cameron (7)**
**Barley Hill Primary School, Thame**


## My Cat Millie

My mini cat is getting fat,
All she does is sleep on her mat,
She likes to go outside every day,
And she loves her own way,
Millie loves to play with me,
And sometimes she climbs a tree,
I kiss her every night,
And say 'Sleep tight'.

**Zoe Chatterton (7)**
**Barley Hill Primary School, Thame**

## Imagine A World Without Movement

Can you imagine a world without moment?
How boring it would be,
To not be able to see the waves crashing on the sea,
Or see the night turn into day,
The world would be simple that way.
No warm or harsh wind weather,
Or times we share together,
Not a growing flower,
Stillness hour on hour.
Imagine a world without moving,
No fun, no laughing, no midnight grooving,
No zooming cars on the motorway,
No changes made day by day,
No athletes racing,
Or playground chasing.
Be happy the world's spinning,
And seasons change with new beginnings,
We can skip, hop, jump and run,
Moving, moving must go on.

**Vicky Kingston (11)**
**Barley Hill Primary School, Thame**


## The Butterfly

The butterfly is a weird type of thing,
It flutters very high,
But when it finds a place to rest,
It's time to say goodbye.

**Imogene Alice Goodman (9)**
**Barley Hill Primary School, Thame**

## My Family's Reactions To Cakes

I love cakes and so does my family,
If you don't believe me wait and see.
My littlest brother crumbles it up,
And after that he drinks from his tiny cup.
My other brother sits in his fluffy dressing gown,
And gobbles all the cake down!
When my little sister eats, she gets very messy,
Just like my friend Jessy.
My daddy asks for a very big slice,
Then all the crumbs go to the mice.
Mummy, well, she saves a huge bite,
And eats it in the middle of the night.
Sadly it is nearly the end of it,
Because the guinea pigs only have a bit.
Last but not least it's me.
As you can tell, for my tea,
I love licking the icing off the cake,
So it is so great that we all love to bake.

**Joely Brewer (7)**
**Barley Hill Primary School, Thame**


## Space Countdown

10 nice spacemen looking for a spoon,
9 planets looking at the moon,
8 rockets going to the hot, hot sun,
7 giant moon monsters looking for a giant bun,
6 spacemen not having much fun,
5 happy aliens having fun playing who can find a great big bun,
4 stars lighting up the night sky,
3 spacemen eating some yummy pie,
2 happy spacemen going to the moon,
1 star playing a lovely tune!

**Isobel Glover (7)**
**Barley Hill Primary School, Thame**

## Flowers

Flowers are pretty, other flowers are witty,
Some make you smile, so stay a while,
Sunflowers make you feel all funny,
Maybe you want a rose,
They have a very good pose,
You could have a daffodil,
They stay so still,
Maybe you've heard of a daisy,
They are so lazy,
Snowdrops glow, bluebells blow,
But who knows where the toadstools grow?

**Annabel Britton (8)**
**Barley Hill Primary School, Thame**


## She's A Thing

When she smiles,
She's a grinning thing,
When she picks her nose,
She's a minging thing,
When she cries,
She's a tearful thing,
When she laughs,
She's a smiley thing,
When she chills,
She's a casual thing,
And when she leaves,
There's no-thing,
To talk about.

**Eleanor Shearwood (10)**
**Barley Hill Primary School, Thame**

## Star Light, Star Bright

Star light, star bright, the star I will see tonight,
I wish I may see the glittery stars shining in the bright, light sky,
It's so bright, I could take it back into planet Earth,
Bye-bye star light, star bright, until next time.
**Casey Stanley (9)**
**Barley Hill Primary School, Thame**


## Cats

If I had a cat, I would stroke him and he would purr
And I would play with him and
He would play with some cotton wool,
And it would go everywhere.
**Hayden Brewer (6)**
**Barley Hill Primary School, Thame**


## Old Trafford

I'd love to go one day,
Up Sir Matt Busby Way,
With the roar of the crowd,
When the volume is loud,
And watch Man U play.

Ooh, it's great to see them score,
And everyone jumps off the floor,
How we could all cheer,
When winning is near,
Oh that wonderful roar.

And when the match is done,
All the family will have fun,
Recalling all the thrills,
As we drive home through the hills,
It's a shame I have never been.
**Samuel Pickup (8)**
**Barley Hill Primary School, Thame**

## Movements In Gymnastics

Spinning, turning and jumping, all those,
Are movements in some way, like touching your toes.
In my acrobatic moves, it feels like flying,
All my moves take effort, with forces applying.

Somersaults, flips, handsprings too,
Splits, tuck-backs, is what some gymnasts do.
Hurdle-step roundoffs, roundoff flics,
These are all movements in gymnastics.

**Cosette Jackson (10)**
**Barley Hill Primary School, Thame**


## My Home

In my home, there is always love and respect,
In my home, there always is joy and peace.

In my home, people always carry beautiful smiles,
In my home, there is God all around.

In my home, there is always food and water for everyone,
My home was a house, but my parents changed it into a *home!*

**Gunishi Nathoo (9)**
**Barley Hill Primary School, Thame**


## Flowers

Pretty flowers, witty flowers,
Small flowers, tall flowers,
Spotty flowers, dotty flowers,
Green flowers, clean flowers,
Gold flowers, old flowers,
I love all flowers.

**Isobel Scarborough (8)**
**Barley Hill Primary School, Thame**

## Where Teachers Keep Their Pets

Mr Hail keeps a quail in his morning mail,
Mrs Oat keeps a goat in her shiny coat,
Mr Bog has a frog, he keeps it by his doorknob,
Mrs Kate keeps a snake with her fruity grapes,
Mrs Hox keeps a fox in her curly locks,
Mr Watt has a cat he keeps in his fancy hat,
Mr Laws keeps a horse in a secret running course,
Mrs Ouse has a mouse she keeps it in her big white house,
Mrs Hickers has a mouse named Flickers and
No one's ever seen where she keeps it!

**Toby Glass (8)**
Beechwood School, Guernsey

## Half-Term

One day to wake up,
One day to have a bun,
One day to finish that homework,
One day to have fun,
One day to go to the park,
One day to talk,
One day to eat lunch,
And have a walk,
One day to go to a game,
One day to play with friends,
Half-term's hardly started,
Before it comes to an end.

**Jamie Hall (7)**
Beechwood School, Guernsey

## Billy The Bully

A bully in the playground,
Was picking on my friend,
He threw his glasses on the floor,
And made them all bend.
My friend then started crying,
And I went to pick him up,
The bully started running until,
Someone tripped him up,
Everyone was laughing,
At the bully on the floor,
The next thing for him was
The headmaster's door.

**Brent Oldfield (7)**
Beechwood School, Guernsey

## The Race

Here I am at the start, I hear the gun.
*Bang!* Off I go! *Run, run, run!*

I'm charging round the track, looking forward,
Never looking back. *Run, run, run!*

I'm going really fast,
Like a rocket blast. *Run, run, run!*

I can see the finish line,
Can I make a record time? *Run, run, run!*

I'm nearly there . . . I've won!
*Yes, yes, yes! Run, run . . . collapse.*

**Nairn Guilbert (8)**
Beechwood School, Guernsey

## Half-Term

One day to BB fight,
One day to play with my friends,
One day to go to a BMX bike track,
One day to go to the cinema,
One day to go to the park and have
Lunch at an all-you-can-eat restaurant,
One day to go into a mine shaft,
One day to go to a museum,
Half-term's hardly started,
Before it comes to an end.

**David Millar (8)**
Beechwood School, Guernsey


## Half-Term

One day for a penalty shoot-out,
One day to go to the park,
One day to go to hockey,
One day to play till it gets dark,
One day to mess around,
One day to play with my bow,
One day to go to cricket,
The swimming gala and golf,
One day to do some homework,
One day to get a loaf,
Half-term's hardly started,
Before it comes to an end.

**Don Harty (7)**
Beechwood School, Guernsey

## The Old School

The old school,
Dark and scary,
I'm in this school,
Frozen with fear,
There are pictures on the walls,
With eyes that watch you,
The old school,
Dark and scary,
Has ghosts of teachers,
And statued students,
With ice-cold skin,
The old school,
Dark and scary,
Is so spooky . . .
I'll never go in again!

**Daniel Davies  (9)**
**Beechwood School, Guernsey**

## My Pet Poem

I have a lovely big black dog,
Bonnie is her name,
She leaps and bounds across the ground,
And I love her just the same.

**Rory Johnson  (7)**
**Beechwood School, Guernsey**

## The Spooky Tower

A spooky tower,
Long and tall,
With creaky banisters,
And crumbling walls,
The gloomy bats . . .
And rats,
Scatter on the cracked floor,
In the shape of a tree,
With its stick branches,
Like a huge hand creeping up on you,
Nothing makes a sound,
Is there something or someone behind me?
I'm sure I heard a creak in the floorboards,
There was an *eek!*
I froze with terror,
And turned around . . .
To face my most dreaded . . . Fear.

**Joshua Shand (9)**
Beechwood School, Guernsey

## Greedy Boy

Once there was a boy,
Who wanted a toy,
He asked for a
Car with a motor,
He asked for a star that shines,
He asked for a big banana,
With big, blue, goggly eyes,
But then he was fed up with all those things,
And gave up.

**Sammy Fowler (8)**
Beechwood School, Guernsey

## Cold Johnny

Cold Johnny lurks in the unused graveyard
With his creaking bones,
Catching his prey when it walks past,
People who walk past there,
Never got heard of ever again,
And cold Johnny still lurks there,
For no one has ever got quite a good
Look at him yet, before he gets you,
And so cold Johnny stays in his grave,
Forever, ever or maybe?

**Teddy Gordon Le-Clerc (8)**
**Beechwood School, Guernsey**

## The Black Wood

The black wood,
Gloomy and dark,
Ash on the floor,
As hot as lava,
I have heard
From the past,
A ferocious beast,
Lived where I lurk right now,
The blazing moon,
Glinting everywhere,
The giant rats,
Scuttling along the hot ash,
Is that the beast scowling close by?
The smoke I see,
Must have blown from his nose,
I wonder if he's heard me
I wonder how big he is
I wonder how fat he is
I wonder if he will eat me.

**Anthony Stokes (9)**
**Beechwood School, Guernsey**

## Castle Of Doom

Castle of doom,
Dark and pale,
No voices anywhere,
Thunder rumbles,
Through my ears,
Bats flutter,
Rats scuttle,
Beaded pictures staring at me,
My heart sinks deeper than the world,
There was a creak,
I heard that people never come out,
I had a chill in my spine,
A day ago, I heard words,
That it will get you,
No one has ever seen,
I heard a snarl,
It got closer,
Suddenly it pounced.

**Jools Houston (9)**
Beechwood School, Guernsey


## In The Forest

Down in the forest,
Gloomy and stark,
Up in the air, the owls hoot,
Down on the ground, the rabbits scoot,
Up in the air and down on the floor,
I saw the shadows of the fox and badger at the door,
Of the bats' dark and gloomy cave,
Will they spot me,
Oh will they?

**Joseph Gillson (8)**
Beechwood School, Guernsey

## The Devil

In my bed I hear,
Something in the corridor,
What should I do?
I am all alone in my bed,
Frozen with fear,
Slowly the door creaks open,
Is there something lurking in the corner?
A huge shadow stands before me,
It swoops down,
What will he do to me?

**George Orton (9)**
Beechwood School, Guernsey


## The Vampire

I sat in my bed,
In the dark,
I saw a man,
A shadow flashed past,
I saw a man,
In my room,
I turned on the lights,
He looked quite friendly,
A sinister grin lay on his face,
But he didn't move an inch,
He glared at my neck,
He showed me his teeth,
They were fangs,
He was a vampire,
A vampire, oh no!

**Bradley Norman (9)**
Beechwood School, Guernsey

## The Vampires

The vampires never die,
They don't care whatever the weather is,
They fly after you,
I see a shadow at my window,
It squeaks open, the curtains tear,
I hide under my covers feeling terrified,
He floats around,
Looking for me,
He slowly lifts the furniture up and puts it back down,
Is he coming nearer? Is he coming nearer?
Lurking in the corners,
He pulls off the covers. He's found me!

**Alexander King (9)**
**Beechwood School, Guernsey**


## The Dark Wood

The dark wood,
Gloomy and noiseless,
The trees rustle,
And the owls hoot,
Shadows are everywhere,
Not even one voice,
But the beasts howl,
The moon shining brightly,
Something howling, do I hear?
Now thunder starts to roar,
Where is the beast?
Will he eat me?

**Oliver Le Marquand (9)**
**Beechwood School, Guernsey**

## What's Creeping In The Dark?

It's time for bed,
I'm feeling scared, something's lurking in the shadows,
Just waiting, just waiting to get me,
I feel a slight chill run down my back,
I want to run to my mum and dad's side,
But my legs won't budge,
I'm on my own, just me and my flesh,
I stay as still as a statue,
Hoping it hasn't seen me.
I reach for my torch . . .
But something blocks me,
Scaly and horrible, just like a snake,
I force my palm through it,
Reaching for the torch,
I flick it on,
Nothing there.

Who is it?
Where is it?
Why is it after me?
I guess I'll never know.

**Elliott Cockett (9)**
Beechwood School, Guernsey


## I Am Everything

I am the yeast in your bread,
I am the motor in your car,
I am the brain in your body,
I am the love in your heart,
I am the honesty in your soul,
I am the fish in the sea,
I am the gas in your cooker,
I am the flour in your cake,
I am the bird in the sky,
I am the god in your beliefs,
I am everything.

**Bertie Charman (11)**
Beechwood School, Guernsey

## The Graveyard

In a dark graveyard
Gloomy and cold
The walls are crumbling
Someone lurks there
I've been told that
People who go there
Are not seen again
Rats scuttle on the ground
But not a sound
Word of a bogeyman
I heard a day ago
No person has been seen
In such a sinister place
An amazing creature lives where I lurk
Flashes of lightning and crashes of thunder roar
Who was it?
What will I do?

**Finley Spence (8)**
Beechwood School, Guernsey


## The Bogeyman

It is a dark night
The bogeyman lurks
In a peculiar place
With a snarl on his face
He waits
He waits
With a snarl on his face
He waits till a child creeps into his lair
His ugly eyes can see ten miles away
The child creeps down
The bogeyman pounces
With a crunch and a swallow
The child is never seen again.

**Jacob Trott (9)**
Beechwood School, Guernsey

## Be My Valentine

Come with me my valentine,
Stay with me and you'll be mine,
Be my sweetheart, night and day,
Be with me in December and May,
You're always tender and kind,
I hope your heart I'll find,
I give you roses, red and white,
And all I see is your wonderful sight,
Come with me to the sunset,
And my heart you'll always get,
Our love is like a never-ending story,
With only joy and glory.

**Conrad Bali & Mats Langseth (10)**
Birralee International School Trondheim, Trondheim, Norway


## The Fantastic World Of Space

Here is an incredible race,
The first one to float in space,
It's also to walk on the moon,
That will happen very soon.
Another goal is Mars,
That is far away in the stars,
Saturn has many rings,
They look like golden strings,
But my dreams are travelling around,
To places no one has found.

**Ludger Albert Moser (10)**
Birralee International School Trondheim, Trondheim, Norway

# The Space

Our home is the Milky Way,
Where our solar system does stay.

The planets orbit the sun in the space,
They move at their own pace,
Some are big, some are small,
The sun itself looks like a fireball.
The sun gives us energy, the light ray,
Without asking us to pay.

The solar system contains other objects,
Asteroids, meteorites and comets.

**Naol Saba (9)**
**Birralee International School Trondheim, Trondheim, Norway**


# Boys

Boys, boys, boys,
Laid-back, cool, weird boys,
Slender, heavy, short boys,
Climbing, boxing, footballing boys,
Rare, careless, splendid boys,
Boys, boys, boys.

**Rebecca Gjaevran Saether (10)**
**Birralee International School Trondheim, Trondheim, Norway**


# Space

Space, space, there is a lot of place for other worlds,
Space, is where you get face to face with an alien,
Who are they?
What do you say?
Are they enemies or friends?
Your comments?
Do they want war or peace?
Can you tell me please.

**Natasha Zotcheva (9)**
**Birralee International School Trondheim, Trondheim, Norway**

## Space

When I look at the stars,
My eyes are full of lights,
I wonder what miracle we can see,
When we have open minds and fantasy.

The moon and the sun,
Look like a prince and a princess,
They are looking after each other,
And never reach each other.

Oh, how much I like to see my shining stars,
When day has gone and night's come by.

**Vanessa Alstad (9)**
**Birralee International School Trondheim, Trondheim, Norway**

## Pigs

Pigs, pigs, pigs,
Pink, muddy, stinky pigs,
Big, fat, enormous pigs,
Stuffing, rolling, grunting pigs,
Guzzling, smelling, dying pigs,
Pigs, pigs, pigs.

**Hedda Nødtvedt (11)**
**Birralee International School Trondheim, Trondheim, Norway**

## Space Poem

Black holes scoff stars,
What for? What's the sense?
No one knows,
Big bad black holes,
Rampage through the space,
Black holes scoff stars,
They leave no trace.

**Marius Haugstad (9)**
**Birralee International School Trondheim, Trondheim, Norway**

## Space

High up there in the sky,
There are stars who would make you die,
Space, space, space, aliens right in front of your face,
Space is a gigantic place,
Planets floating high up there,
No one knows exactly where,
Space is a wonderful big place,
Dreams get true and life gets new.

**Camilla Steen (10)**
Birralee International School Trondheim, Trondheim, Norway

## Ghosts

Ghosts, ghosts, ghosts,
Small, scary, white ghosts,
Wide, skinny, tall ghosts,
Sleeping, scaring, killing ghosts,
Bony, dead, cold ghosts,
Ghosts, ghosts, ghosts.

**Martine Brun (11)**
Birralee International School Trondheim, Trondheim, Norway

## Space

Space,
Is a wonderful place,
You have Pluto, Neptune, Uranus, Venus and Mars,
Mercury, Saturn, Earth, Jupiter and stars,
Space,
Is a wonderful place.

**Adrian Langseth (9)**
Birralee International School Trondheim, Trondheim, Norway

# My Magic Box
*(Based on 'Magic Box' by Kit Wright)*

I will put in my box . . .

My best friend Hazel
with her pony Whirl
To have for company.

Paper and pens
to draw pictures
colour and write.

I will put in my box . . .

Charlie and Ellen Whitaker
to get riding tips from
especially show jumping ones.

A professional, special
computer to play
do work and learn.

I will put in my box . . .

My mum, dad, my brother
and my whole English
family for cuddles and to talk to.

A pocket camera with
mega, mega pixels to take
pictures of everyone.

I will put in my box . . .

Pippa, Joey and Olaf
To ride, jump and cuddle
all cute, all for me.

Books about animals
so I can read whenever I want
and study as well.

I will put in my box . . .

Pizza, chips, a chocolate bar
and some fresh fruit smoothies
to eat and to drink.

Big cats and a huge chunk
of wilderness so they don't
get extinct.

I will put in my box . . .

A big ménage show jumps
and fields,
to ride in and over.

All of my friends Megan
Vikky, Laura J and more
so we can have lots of fun.

**Laura Pratley (11)**
**Blakesley CE Primary School, Towcester**

## My Magic Box
*(Based on 'Magic Box' by Kit Wright)*

I will put in my box . . .
My pony Mel
And a ménage
So I can ride him inside it.

I will put in my box . . .
Mashed potato
Sausage and beans
A never-ending supply

I will put in my box . . .
A genie
With a magic lamp
For three wishes.

I will put in my box . . .
Art stuff
And some books to read
To keep me occupied.

I will put in my box . . .
A computer and a camera
To download pictures from.

I will put in my box . . .
My cousin Georgia
And her pony Jakeub
So we can have some fun.

I will put in my box . . .
My rabbit (Peter)
And my cat (Blossom)
To keep me company.

I will put in my box . . .
My brother and
My mum and dad
The family I love.

**Katie Noble (11)**
**Blakesley CE Primary School, Towcester**


## My Magic Box
*(Based on 'Magic Box' by Kit Wright)*

I will put in my box . . .
A house for me to live in,
Some pasta for me to eat,
Some elderflower cordial to drink.

I will put in my box . . .
My dog for someone to play with,
My friends for someone to talk to,
My family to keep me company.

**Simon Walker (11)**
**Blakesley CE Primary School, Towcester**

## My Magic Box
*(Based on 'Magic Box' by Kit Wright)*

I will put in my magic box . . .
My plasma screen TV so I can play on the Wii
Or a PS3 so it can beat the Wii
And a big bad hall so I can play basketball.

I will put in my magic box . . .
A nice big fox so I don't get chickenpox
Or an Xbox 360 so I can play 'Halo 3'
A bit of the sea and have a cup of tea.

I will put in my magic box . . .
A dusty lamp for three wishes so I don't have to do the dishes
A DS Lite so I can see at night
A load of meats so I can have a feast.

**Aidan Louw (10)**
**Blakesley CE Primary School, Towcester**


## My Magic Box
*(Based on 'Magic Box' by Kit Wright)*

In my magic box I will put . . .
My cat who will keep me warm,
My mum and dad so I can have a computer,
My dog so I can play with him,
My hamster so fluffy and warm.

In my magic box I will put . . .
Mrs Henson so she can teach me,
All my teddy bears,
Books so I can read them,
Friends so I can play with them.

In my magic box I will put . . .
PJs so when I go to sleep I can wear them,
Food so I can eat,
Lots of fruit so I can eat them,
Paper and pencils so I can draw.

**Louise Duffy (10)**
**Blakesley CE Primary School, Towcester**

## The Magic Box
*(Based on 'Magic Box' by Kit Wright)*

In my magic box I will put . . .
My dog Pippa to play with me and keep me company
My family to keep me safe and healthy
My house to keep me warm in the harshest of weather.

I will put in my magic box . . .
All of my friends to play with and talk to
Willy Wonka's chocolate factory with an endless supply
Of everything in there so I never go hungry.

I will put in my magic box . . .
A kind dentist to keep my teeth healthy from Willy Wonka's
                                            chocolate factory
A paramedic tent to stop me from dying
A TV with Sky+.

I will put in my magic box . . .
A rugby pitch and a ball so I can play
A Guinness Book of World Records 2008
And a Wii with all of the games.

**Vincenzo Pratley (10)**
**Blakesley CE Primary School, Towcester**

## The Magic Box
*(Based on 'Magic Box' by Kit Wright)*

I will put in my magic box . . .
Meg's good life to keep me company,
My family to look after me,
Freckles so that I can ride him.

I will put in my magic box . . .
Mrs Henson to teach me,
Sooty to have fun and play with,
A clock so that I can tell the time.

I will put in my magic box . . .
My bed so I can go to sleep,
My cuddly panda to cuddle up to,
Polar bears so they do not go extinct.

I will put in my magic box . . .
Clothes so that I can keep warm,
Drinks so I won't die of thirst,
Food so that I can eat.

**Natalya Zajko (10)**
**Blakesley CE Primary School, Towcester**

## The Magic Box
*(Based on 'Magic Box' by Kit Wright)*

I will put in my box . . .
My nan, mum and brother
I will put in my hamster Speedy
And my rabbit, Peter Rabbit.

I will put in my box . . .
My 'Race for Life' medal and key ring
And the 'run for the children' medal.

I will put in my box . . .
My ballet medal
And my ballet and tap certificates.

I will put in my box . . .
My ballet gifts for doing so well
And my favourite teacher Mrs Henson
And her pet Sooty.

**Abbey-Anne Gyles (10)**
Blakesley CE Primary School, Towcester


## The Wonderful Wizard

There was a wizard with long silver hair
If you go near his potions he'll shout out, 'Beware!'
Full of frogs' legs and toadstools and other such things
He will have anything, even bats' wings
He lives in a castle with dungeons and dragons
He travels around in bright coloured wagons
This wizard makes such wonderful creations
I'm not sure how he does it saying silly incantations.

**Rebecca Cox (9)**
Castel Primary School, Guernsey

## When I Was Boy

When I was a boy
I remember
spring picnics in the garden
with sandwiches and cakes
Sunny meadows in the summer
with ice-cool lakes
A bed of leaves in the autumn
and cool crisp air
And in the winter home-made angels
with silky golden hair

I had memories in autumn
I had memories in spring
But when I was a boy
Christmas was my
favourite thing.

**Ewan Edward Reynolds (9)**
Castel Primary School, Guernsey

## Imagine If . . .

I magine if I hated cats
M ice and rats
A nimals of all sorts, argh!
G olly that would be a pain
I magine if Ruby was the same
N iamh as well, golly what a shame
E lise loves them all, not so bad after all

I magine if we all loved them
F amilies can be funny
   Just imagine if . . .

**Sophie Le Feuvre (8)**
Castel Primary School, Guernsey

## My Phantom Pussy Cat

There was a pitch-black pussy cat,
His eyes an emerald-green,
The only times I saw him,
Was in my nightly dreams,
Pouncing on a scuttling rat,
Standing stiffly alert,
But he wasn't mine at all,
And that bit really hurt,
But then we went to the pet shop,
And I found my perfect pet,
My lovely phantom pussy cat,
Is the one that I will get,
Because my phantom pussy cat,
Meant all the world to me,
I got one just like he looked,
A velvety black pussy.

**Lota Nwokolo (10)**
Castel Primary School, Guernsey


## If . . .

If petals were dates
I'd send you flowers
If raindrops were hugs
I'd send you showers
If minutes were kisses
I'd send you hours
If waves were wishes
I'd send you the sea
If love was a person
I'd send you me!

**Katie Anderson (10)**
Castel Primary School, Guernsey

## The Wind

The wind whistles down in the dark alleyway
Ladies walking past with umbrellas turning inside out
When the wind whistles.

The wind whistles on the beach
Blowing sand and seaweed in our eyes
The children cry
When the wind whistles.

The wind whistles in the park
Children playing in the arc are cold and sad
When the wind whistles.

A monster jumps out walking the streets
Finding little kids to eat
He kills anything that comes close to his warts on his nose.

As the wind blows he runs, he goes
The wind is our saviour.

**Robyn Munro (8)**
**Castel Primary School, Guernsey**


## The Lion

The lion of the jungle,
Ferocious, mean lion.
So run,
Run away,
Far away.
Don't come back again.
I stroll around looking for prey,
On sunny days I graze in the sun,
On windy days I lay in my den.
So beware of . . . the lion of the jungle.

**Bernice Saunders (7)**
**Castel Primary School, Guernsey**

## A Snowy Christmas

Santa's coming
Children sleeping
Bringing presents
Reindeers leading
Snowing gently
Reindeers freezing
Robins flying
Merry Christmas.

**Kirsty Standring (9)**
Castel Primary School, Guernsey

## Wedding Day

This is the day when two hearts become one,
When a smile is painted in the sky,
All worries washed away,
Trailing their troubles behind them as they follow their hearts
down the aisle,
And that first kiss will be the kiss that carries their love on forever.
For on that one day, and that one day only,
The world is theirs.

**Skye Turner (11)**
Edward Field CP School, Kidlington

## Anger

Black and grey, like a bird it swoops,
A burning poison flowing through you,
It smells like smoke rising to the top,
It is a fire jumping and spitting,
A fiery flame leaping,
Boiling lava in your throat.

**Edward Hopkin (10)**
Edward Field CP School, Kidlington

## Dizzily

Dizzily the Catherine wheel spins round and round,
Dizzily the roller coaster curls round the loops,
Dizzily the spinning top keels over,
Dizzily the ballerina turns on her toe.

Dizzily the dragon drifts round its lair,
Dizzily the daft drunken man staggers up the hill,
Dizzily the propeller directs the plane - but dizziest of all
The imaginative thoughts that race through our minds.

**Kieran Kilcoyne (8)**
Edward Field CP School, Kidlington

## Loneliness

Loneliness is grey
Tears and hurts all in its spell
Tastes like a single mouldy apple
Ruins other people's lives
Like smoke coming out of a burning house
A child lost and forgotten far, far away
'I wish I wasn't on my own,'
The voice spoke from the lonely mouth of a child
Then silence broke out
Nothing was heard, nothing at all
It feels soft and tender
Loneliness haunts you!

**Emily Hurdley (11)**
Edward Field CP School, Kidlington

## Under The Water

Arriving at the harbour,
Boat screaming excitedly, eager to go,
Up slithers the sail like a cloud in the sky,
*Grrrr* growls the engine, roaring to go.

Over the water, over the deep blue sea,
A bright sapphire sheet of silk,
Dark patches, light patches.

Boat ready to stop,
*Grrrr* . . . as it steadily slows down,
Ready to stop . . . stopping . . . stopped.

The suit is grabbed onto my body,
Wet and hard to slip on,
Bright yellow, a mix of black,
The tank and away we go.

Wriggling, sitting, waiting . . . waiting,
Sitting excitedly on the metal grey steps,
Slip on flippers and off we go.

Into the depths of the underwater kingdom,
A cobalt-coloured sky all around me.

Tiny fish, huge fish, fish all around me,
Sharks! They're harmless,
Multicoloured coral, all different types,
Everything I could wish for.

After the dive I didn't feel alone,
We talked about what we saw,
Off slithers the suit.

Arriving at the harbour,
Getting off the boat,
Down comes the sail like the cloud floating away,
*Grrrr* growls the engine, as it shuts down and dies.

**Martha Cook (10)**
Edward Field CP School, Kidlington

# Sound

Sound stretches idly, wakes and tumbles out of bed
Creeping around the corner
Salaciously sleazily
I turn around
It isn't there -
Why is it stalking me?
But still it carries on
Humiliating me
Tagging round like a dog on a lead

Sound screams out in anger
As sharp as vinegar
A lion -
Roaring with displeasure
I try with might to ignore it
But it grabs my ears with clenched fists
I'm living in a nightmare
I'm being swallowed in a whirlpool of sound

Why is it ringing endlessly?
Bouncing off walls
Dodging and diving through people's feet
My ears swim in sound
Sound scuttles along the uneven paving like spiders
Sounds creep up the walls like ivy
Sound is a gaping crocodile's mouth
Caving in on you
It is a poisonous snake
Releasing its venom
Sound is a headache which
Refuses to go.

**Genevieve Tomes (10)**
Edward Field CP School, Kidlington

## Candle

A puddle of wax reluctantly gripping on to the edge
The wick bends over like an elderly age man
It sits on the side lonely and dull
It smells of fresh air reaching to the sky
The northern lights gliding around the wick
It's like a bomb full of colours
Coats of sweat sticking to its body

The flame waves and jumps like a crazy chicken
It's soundless and timid
It makes you feel relaxed and calm
Its enemy is wind, it picks on it and bullies it
Until its gigantic flame has gone and gasps its last breath.

**Darryl Salmon (10)**
Edward Field CP School, Kidlington


## Skiing

Sweet sound of gondola as you fly over trees,
Bullet down the slalom to the singing chairlift,
Summit approaching to my ice-cold eyes,
Button lift closing in on me,
Humming on a gentle ride.

The skills park sleeping - still but not dead,
Hearts pounding on the deadly grind,
Leap with unbelievable speed,
A red arrow speeding through the air,
Loop the loop - like you just don't care,
Speed down the slope like a grizzly bear.

Avalanches crashing and chasing me,
Falling snow pinching in the cold,
Rocks approaching to break my knee,
Speedily skiing supremely.

**Toby Cole (10)**
Edward Field CP School, Kidlington

## Loneliness

Loneliness is black,
Creeping over you like ivy up a wall.
It tastes sickly and sour,
Making your taste buds tingle.
It's a ghost.
A haunting spirit
Killing you.
A black hole,
Leading to nowhere.
Fills you with hatred for yourself,
And others.
'I creep up and fill you with sadness,
Making you feel sick,
Make your skin crawl!'
'No, leave me alone,
You're killing me, killing me,
All I wanted was to be noticed.'
It slides and slithers,
Into every inch of your body.
Loneliness is a horrid emotion to feel.

**Rachel Barrett (11)**
Edward Field CP School, Kidlington

## Anger

Anger is a giant pool of cold blood,
As horrid as hot mushy Brussels sprouts,
It sounds like a bonfire exploding the wrong way,
It tastes like burnt burger left for ages.
The cause of destruction,
Anger is as dark as cold oil,
Feeling you would explode any minute,
It looks as disgusting as a squashed apple and custard pie,
Smells like burnt steak,
Destroying people's minds like a giant bowling ball.
Anger is as heavy as a 10 tonne brick.

**Kamran Afzal (10)**
Edward Field CP School, Kidlington

## Loneliness

Grey dust flew around me,
The taste was plain, plain as paper.
I sat in the smallest corner thinking . . .
(Like I was a tiger locked away)
I've never had this feeling before.
Flickers of brick travelled into my mouth,
Why was I the forgotten one?
Blackness covered my eyes - hands cold as ice.

Squeals in my ear,
Bats flew over my head.
I was lost in my own world!
My heart thumping
Harder . . .
Harder . . .
My face dropped,
I fell,
I was really lost!
My head spun.
Eyes grew around me,
I fell in pain.

**Phoebe Knight (10)**
Edward Field CP School, Kidlington

## Joy

Joy is bright purple,
Tasting as juicy as ripe berries,
With its secret essence of lavender.
It's a field of germinating bluebells
Dancing in the moonlight,
Singing its sweet song echoing in the sunset,
Wraps you up tight in its purple duvet.
It calls out, 'Hooray!' Jumping merrily,
Swimming in the pool of wind,
Joy is sensational.

**Danielle Hollis (11)**
Edward Field CP School, Kidlington

## Creeping Mouse

Silent scamper,
Scary noise,
Claws on the floor,
Silence broken,
Tiny squeak.

Creeping up on you,
Blackness calls,
Minute whisper,
Loud scream,
Walls creeping in.

Driving you mad,
Sneaking towards the door,
Weird noises,
Horrid scary sounds,
Wonders where you are?

Silent scamper,
Scary noise,
Claws on the floor,
Silence broken,
Tiny squeak.

**Jade Ghanbary (10)**
Edward Field CP School, Kidlington

## Fear

The chilling work of Satan
As disgusting as tomato pie
Living in the middle of nowhere
The cause of suspense and destruction
Ability to shape shift
Everyone falls victim
One second you are unaware of the circumstances
The next you are petrified!
There are no survivors . . .

**Magnus Taylor (10)**
Edward Field CP School, Kidlington

## Agitation

Agitation is red,
Agitation is a pool of blood,
Agitation sounds like the red-hot pits of Hell,
Looks like the fat Devil,
Smells like a gigantic bonfire,
Tastes like a crispy burger,
Feels like a burning stick,
Agitation is life-threatening.

**Robbie Jacques (11)**
Edward Field CP School, Kidlington

## A House Awakes

Door opening, mouth yawning
Fire on house, coughing
Window ledge, eyelashes
Lights turn on, house wakes up
Putting post in the letter box
Putting food in your mouth
Curtains open, house comes awake
Door mat waving its tongue
The door porch, teeth
Door opening, house smiling
Gate moving, house waving
Curtains open and close
House blinks goodbye
The door frame is a mouth with the teeth in it
The roof of the house is the head of a human being.

**Joshua Goddard (9)**
Flore CE Primary School, Northampton

## A Waking House

In the morning the
house awakes the plants
to see the sun waving. The door
yawns to await the tongue of the house
which reaches the nose-like gate, the eyes open
to see the blinding sun. If you go in this house you
will hear the gargle of the toilet flushing
and the sneezing sound of the shower drains
your mind then the smoky smell of the
house ears, down in the heart of the house
it burns. The house waves with its greenish
arms, the eyebrows of the house twitch and
The house dozes, swallows and burns fiery.

**Lorna Butler (10)**
Flore CE Primary School, Northampton

## Ostrich Kennings

Dirt-head
Face-scratcher
Ground-digger
Egg-layer
Fast-runner
Food-grabber
Mud-tredder
Feathered-back
Stretched-neck.

**Karampreet Kaur (10)**
Flore CE Primary School, Northampton

## The Day Of Awakening

Smoke shows its memo of yesterday, thinking so toughly.
Roof tiles are messier placed because of its ageing.
Its beautiful sapphire eyes glow in the morning light.
The pretty coloured curtains open their eye blankets.
The door yawns loudly wakening the sleepy creak inside.
The neck getting ready for visitors coming to visit.
The car engine creeping up its pebbly back.

**Joanna Bucknall (9)**
Flore CE Primary School, Northampton

## Cat Kennings

Sharp-clawer
High-jumper
Six-whiskers
Happy-purr
Good-climber
Soft-fur.

**Haydn Groves (9)**
Flore CE Primary School, Northampton

## Leaves Playing

The leaves skip to the ground with laughter
Like they've been waiting for weeks
To be free
Blow with the wind
With their friends
Dance, blow, skip
Leaves green, yellow, brown!

**Molly Smith (10)**
Flore CE Primary School, Northampton

## A House Awakes

In the morning . . .
The house starts to awake
The blinds open their sleepy eyes
The smoky arms of the chimney stretch
Windows open their eyes
The kettle groans loudly
The toilet flush sneezes
The rain starts to run
Gravel brushes its teeth
The car's engine coughs.

**Gemma Jones (11)**
Flore CE Primary School, Northampton

## Fox

Mice-predator
Sly-sneaker
Green-eyes
Fantastic-digger
Chicken-robber
Brown-fur.

**Jack Walton (10)**
Flore CE Primary School, Northampton

## Badger

Brilliant-digger
Black-creature
Fantastic-digger
Blind-creature
Worm-eater
Sharp-nails
Sharp-teeth.

**Jacob Ogden (9)**
Flore CE Primary School, Northampton

## A House Awakes . . .

When the house awakes, the curtains draw back
like windows opening their eyes.
When the fire's lit, it turns on the brain of the house
to get ready for the day.
When the door's mouth opens, it yawns like a new day has started.
When the path leads to the house, its tongue draws in from yawning.
When the eyes blink slowly, it's like the curtains are being drawn
to go to sleep.
When the curtains are being drawn, the eyes blink slowly,
beginning to go to sleep.
When the house goes to sleep it snores like a creaky floor
as the curtains are drawn to go to bed.

**Charley Rideout (10)**
Flore CE Primary School, Northampton


## The House Awakes

Early in the morning the house
Awakes ready to begin a new day.
The blazing bright light turns on
As the brain switches itself on.
As the burning fire is lit the house
Coughs out cloudy smoke.
The wooden door opens as the house yawns.
The tap runs, slimy water pouring out,
The house is dribbling.
As the fire crackles the house sings to itself.
The wind charges through the window
As the house breathes in.
The green ivy grows on the head of the house,
The house has grown its hair.
The windows are closed, the lights are switched off
And the house goes to sleep.

**Emily Cousins (10)**
Flore CE Primary School, Northampton

## Early In The Morning

Early in the morning
the windows open their eyes
the door yawns as it is being opened
and the stairs
swallow as people head down them.
The pane of
the windows rattle as its teeth are being
cleaned
by the electric
lights and
the fire is
snoring.
The doors
of the
wardrobe
are blinking.
People are
its food
as they head
down the landing.

**Ben Kingston (10)**
**Flore CE Primary School, Northampton**


## The Famous Horse Kennings

Mane-tosser
Hoof-clopper
Human-rider
Fast-glider
Oat-eater
Foot-beater
What do you get?
A horse!

**Ellie Cockerill (9)**
**Flore CE Primary School, Northampton**

## A House Awakes

Early in the morning
The house opens its eyes as the lights switch on
The house gargles as the tap runs
Early in the morning
The house swallows as the post comes in the letter box
The floorboards creak as the house groans
Early in the morning
The chimney coughs as the smoke comes out
The wind blows and the house shivers
The house yawns as the door opens
Early in the morning.

**Jemma Mason (11)**
**Flore CE Primary School, Northampton**


## Lion - Haiku

A lion creeps up,
Sharp claws waiting to attack
Its prey, the zebra.

**Reuben Lownes (9)**
**Flore CE Primary School, Northampton**


## The Wolf

Night-howler
Teeth-glinter
Meat-hunter
Sly-prowler
High-pouncer
Moonlight-stalker.

**Alex Bucknall (11)**
**Flore CE Primary School, Northampton**

## Dolphin

Wave-splasher
Deep sea-diver
Graceful-jumper
Net-poisoner
Cute-cup winner
Water-sprayer
Fish-eater
Beauty-seeker
Nose-squeaker
Amazing-dancer
Elegant-glider.

**Bryony Mead (10)**
**Flore CE Primary School, Northampton**

## The T-Rex

Meat-eater
Sharp-teeth
Death-lizard
Scaly-skin
Giant-feet
Prehistoric-creature.

**George Underwood (11)**
**Flore CE Primary School, Northampton**

## Honeybee

Air-dancer
Pollen-collector
Honey-maker
Bottom-stinger
Yellow-striper
Royal-server
Flower-friend.

**Amy Welbourne (11)**
**Flore CE Primary School, Northampton**

## War

Bullet-parade
Camouflage-cannon
Death-detector
Blood-battle
Violent-killer
Deadly-fighter
Freedom-decider
Dangerous-disaster
Bomb-blaster.

**Alexander Morehen (10)**
Flore CE Primary School, Northampton

## Penguin

Belly-slider
Deep sea-diver
Fish-hunter
Water-conqueror
Egg-carrier
Seal-escaper
Walking-waddler.

**Elliot Wilde (10)**
Flore CE Primary School, Northampton

## Tiger - Haiku

Silent like a mouse
Angry like a dinosaur
Stalking its dinner.

**Jake Howard (11)**
Flore CE Primary School, Northampton

## A House Awakes

Early in the morning . . .
  Windows open their tired eyes
    The door yawns lazily
      The sink throat gargles loudly
        Tree arms wave at people passing by
          The letter box begins to sing
            The porch groans
              The body shivers
                The path tongue wobbles
                The chimney coughs.

**Abigail Wright (10)**
**Flore CE Primary School, Northampton**

## King Of The Jungle - Haiku

King of the jungle
Lies upon the horizon
Waiting for someone.

**Sam Norman (10)**
**Flore CE Primary School, Northampton**

## Tiger Kennings

Sharp-teeth
Fast-runner
Meat-eater
High-jumper
Fast-climber
Good-catcher.

**Alex Salmons (9)**
**Flore CE Primary School, Northampton**

## Anger

Anger is red like an erupting volcano
Rushing down and down.
It's as spicy as chilli
Burning your mouth - *hot, hot, hot!*
It smells like smoke
From a blazing fire.
It looks like scarlet blood
Pouring from your heart.
It sounds like evil laughter
Running through your mind.
It feels like rough rugged boulders
Tearing at your skin
Until . . . you're .. . . dead . . .

**Yasin Tall (10)**
Gilberdyke Primary School, Brough

## Hate

It looks like fiery orange and red.
Hate tastes as horrible as burnt ash.
It smells like a puff of big black smoke.
Hate looks like a big explosion.
It sounds like a nuclear bomb going off.
Hate feels as sharp as spiky nails scratching you.

**Angus Harvey (9)**
Gilberdyke Primary School, Brough

## Love

Love is pink like Turkish delight on marshmallows.
Chocolate creams explode with love.
Love smells like cake on my birthday.
It looks like leaves in awesome autumn.
It sounds like trees whooshing around
And feels like a fur collar around your neck.

**Shannon Rastrick (9)**
Gilberdyke Primary School, Brough

## Fear

Fear is a fearful dark green colour,
It tastes like a disgusting dollop of green sprouts when you eat them,
It smells like a slice of black burnt toast,
Fear is creeping through a dark forest,
It looks like a bag of blood,
It sounds like the shooting of a shotgun,
It feels like a sharp knife about to kill you.

**Katie Last (9)**
Gilberdyke Primary School, Brough

## Happiness

Happiness is like a bright bouncy ball
It tastes like a swirly lollipop being licked
It smells like wild pink candyfloss in a swishing swashy candy machine
It looks like massive hot air balloons taking off like an eagle
Also sounds like dolphins squealing with joy
And feels like shells so smooth on your skin.

**Amy Woodward (9)**
Gilberdyke Primary School, Brough

## Love

Love is peace,
Love is calm,
Love is a very beautiful charm
And tastes just like strawberry milkshake.
It looks like a fluttering fairy way up high in the sky.
It smells like sherbet scattered around, mmm just smell that sherbet on the ground.
Love is silky soft just waiting to be felt.
Love is our heart and gives pride and happiness to everyone.

**Danielle Hardgrave (10)**
Gilberdyke Primary School, Brough

## Excitement Is A . . .

Excitement is a roller coaster,
Bobbin' up and down,
Or how about a tiny toaster
When it's burning away?

Excitement is like a gigantic blue well done,
Happy and proud,
Is the feeling
When you've won.

Excitement is a holiday
When you're driving there,
Excitement is a happy hooray
On a summer morning.

**Tom Shanks (10)**
Gilberdyke Primary School, Brough


## Anger Poem!

Anger is as hot as fire
Spreading over the land.
It is as fierce as a wrestler
Attacking its prey.
It smells of the dead
Lying in its grave for ever and ever
Resting the night away
For many nights and days.
The rats like it in a lot of ways.
Anger looks like blood
Swimming in a flood.
The old will die
The young will starve
Like the sound of a great big roar.

**Joe Huntley (9)**
Gilberdyke Primary School, Brough

## Happiness

Happiness is yellow like a fluffy chick,
Tastes like strawberries sweet in the summer,
Smells like a rose sitting in the sun,
Looks like a lamb leaping around,
Sounds like birds singing in the trees,
Feels like wool on my granny's sweater.

**Megan Malcolmson (10)**
Gilberdyke Primary School, Brough

## Anger

Anger is roaring red
It tastes like strawberries
It smells like an apple abandoned by the tree
It looks like burning bright lava
It sounds like a World War II bomb exploding
It feels like rough sandpaper.

**Joseph Allen (10)**
Gilberdyke Primary School, Brough

## Fear

Fear is a dark night
It tastes like cold greasy chips
It smells like shoe-swallowing swamp
It looks like a damp eerie house
It sounds like a scary storm raging through the world
It feels like being totally alone
And fear sneaks up on you and gives you a
Fright!

**Joe Sefton (10)**
Gilberdyke Primary School, Brough

## Love

Pink is love.
It tastes like rosy red strawberries.
It smells like strong daffodils.
Love looks like a fluffy cloud in the shape of a heart.
Love sounds like the waves coming to shore.
It feels like a summery breeze.

**Molly Brown (10)**
Gilberdyke Primary School, Brough

## Dreams

I lay awake on a cold dark night,
There was no sound, there was no light.
I close my eyes and tried to sleep,
I even tried counting sheep.

It wasn't until I got to twenty-three,
It suddenly occurred to me,
That I had fallen into a dream
And was floating down a stream.

I dreamt I was in a field of corn,
I dreamt of when I was being born,
I dreamt of swimming down the Nile,
I dreamt of playing with my friends a while.

I dreamt of flying over a lake,
All of a sudden I was awake!

**Alex Downes (10)**
Harwell Primary School, Didcot

## I Know A Vampire

I know a vampire that lives downstairs
I know a vampire that has pet bears
I know a vampire that has crazy hair
I know a vampire that goes to the fair

I know a vampire that lives down the street
I know a vampire that has crazy feet
I know a vampire that eats meat
I know a vampire that has a room without heat

I know a vampire that lives on my road
I know a vampire who carries a heavy load
I know a vampire who owns a pet toad
I know a vampire who knew he was owed

I know a vampire who lives in a hall
I know a vampire who wasn't there at all.

**James Hartley (11)**
Harwell Primary School, Didcot

## My Poem

This is my poem
Do you think I should make it rhyme?
Maybe I should do it about my pets
Or maybe just one subject
Oh no, I haven't made it rhyme and I've haven't got much time
I could do it about school
Well maybe not
What about the good things in life
Maybe music
I still don't have much time
Oh what could I write this poem about?

**Anna Hobin (10)**
Harwell Primary School, Didcot

## My Dream

I said goodnight,
I went to bed,
I closed my eyes
And I dreamt.

I dreamt I was flying
Through the midnight sky,
On a white horse called Star
Past the big white moon.

I flew past the Milky Way,
I floated in the air,
I drifted into outer space
And I so wonder why.

There are bad dreams with witches
And evil queens with nasty stews,
Oh bad dreams you are mean
And I really hate you.

It's morning now
And I'm awake,
Those dreams were very weird,
I'll think of them today.

**Charlotte Adams (10)**
**Harwell Primary School, Didcot**


## Summer

S unshine
U nhappy people are scarce
M oney that you spend on ice creams
M erry people that you see playing on the beach
E veryone is having fun,
R eally lovely summer.

**Rosie Fishburn (9)**
**Harwell Primary School, Didcot**

## Sweets

Gummy bears, pink and green,
The most amazing things you've ever seen,
Gumdrops, pear-shaped and candy sticks curled,
When I think of them, I'm in a different world.

Valentine's Day,
Takes my heart away,
When I look into the sweet shops
And see a chocolate box.

But my favourite sweet, better than dazzling sunbeams,
To me they're like crystalised dreams,
The flavour lasts forever, they're the best treat,
It's the edible rainbow that is the simple boiled sweet.

But there is one sweet that I cannot stand,
Compared to the other sweets, it's not nearly as grand,
The one thing I would not miss,
Is that evil liquorice!

**Elinor Clarke (11)**
**Harwell Primary School, Didcot**


## The Mystery Guest

Chest tickler
Nose picker
Everywhere throw upper
(When he's got a cold)
Shoulder poker
Hair scratcher
Tummy hugger
My brother.

**Joshua Samuel Buttery (9)**
**Harwell Primary School, Didcot**

## Rainbow

R ainbow, colourful things, full of happiness
A nimals part of nature, colours of the rainbow
I sland, many colours, they're all over the world
N ow the future is ahead of us
B oats, fishing boats take parts of our nature away
O ut, rainbows are outside and in
W indows help light get in your home and schools
and many other places.

**Charlotte Grocutt (10)**
**Harwell Primary School, Didcot**


## Spring

S is for sun, shining through the clouds.
P is for people running and laughing happily.
R is for run in the sun, skip and whistle.
I is for imagination. Can you imagine anything so pretty?
N is for nest, a tiny chick chirps for its food.
G is for being grateful for the lovely times we have in spring.

**Gemma Tankard (9)**
**Harwell Primary School, Didcot**


## Quietly

Quietly I listen for the stars
Quietly I read my book
Quietly the spaceship goes to Mars
Quietly I hang my coat on the hook
Quietly the cat stalks its prey
Quietly I drift away.

**Annie Vickers (9)**
**Harwell Primary School, Didcot**

## When Will It End?

Where am I? What place is this? What will they do? When will it end?

At first I thought it would be fun,
But now I can't even eat a crumb,

It is so wet and cold in the trenches,
I wish I was sat at my old school benches,

I hate to see my mates in pain,
I wonder what the country will gain,

It's so horrible out here,
I wish I was in the local having a beer,

I don't think I could shed another tear,
I can't wait to see my dear,

Even though it might not show,
I really want to come home with my friends in tow,

I used to take things for granted,
But now I, my wife and my kids are parted.

Where am I? What place is this? What will they do? When will it end?

**Jessica Brady (10)**
Harwell Primary School, Didcot

## Adventures

A is for advancing into a forest.
D is for danger ahead of you.
V is for visibility in the murky waters.
E is for expedition, searching for lost treasure.
N is for nature in that we find things.
T is for teamwork to help each other.
U is for undertaking new challenges.
R is for risk-taking for the benefit of your team.
E is for experience to help others.
S is for support by encouraging others.

**Jack Constant (10)**
Harwell Primary School, Didcot

## My Eight Wonders Of The World

My eight wonders of the world aren't 'great mountains'
Or 'amazing rivers',
There're the things we take for granted
And things we don't really appreciate.

My eight wonders of the world are:

*Friends* because they are always there for you
when you need a helping hand

*Family* because what would we do without them!

*Happiness* because otherwise we'd always be sad,
lonely and miserable

*Love* because without it no one would have any feelings
for each other

*Kindness* because like happiness and love, how could we
live without it?

Senses because what would the world mean if you couldn't see,
hear, taste, touch or smell

*Dreams* because without them what would life be like if we didn't
watch those little movies in our head while we sleep

And last but definitely not least, *the world we live in,* without it
we'd be nothing!

**Laura Passau (10)**
**Harwell Primary School, Didcot**

## 1966

The England team
In black and white
Came running onto the field
Desperate, desperate, desperate
To hold the winning shield.

The German team
Were here to play
They would put up a fight
On the Wembley scene
England showed their might.

Then the whistle blew
Phew! That was great
2-0 to England and only half-time
The German team still had time
Of their victory goal they did a mime.

Then Germany scored a goal
Could England hold on?
The whistle blew, only injury time to go
2 minutes, 1 minute, 5, 4, 3, 2, 1 . . .
England had barely lifted a toe.

And we all know that
Everyone started down and up
Victory!
England had won
The World Cup!

**Robert Dickens (11)**
**Harwell Primary School, Didcot**

## Alone

He sits there alone;
Waiting,
Staying in the corner,
He sees his friends, his family,
His dog,
Gone;
Destruction everywhere.
No one ever comes,
No one ever has,
It's pointless,
Life is pointless,
Then, a stroke of happiness,
A smiling face
And a hand,
A helping hand,
His heart lifts,
The first smile in years!

**Eleanor Turner (11)**
**Harwell Primary School, Didcot**

## Silent Things

The wind whispering.
Ice glistening in the sun.
The breath of a rhino.
My tummy grasping for food.
A mouse's tail wriggling.
A pencil desperate to write.
A wand sleeping in its case.

**Theo Jones (9)**
**Leighfield Primary School, Uppingham**

## Attraction

I'm as attracted to you as a baby to crying
I'm as attracted to you as a mum to sighing

I'm as attracted to you as a dog to a bone
I'm as attracted to you as a girl to the phone

I'm as attracted to you as rubbish to a bin
I'm as attracted to you as a fish to its fin

I'm as attracted to you as a mouse to its cheese
I'm as attracted to you as mud to knees

I'm as attracted to you as a footballer to a ball
I'm as attracted to you as backstroke in a pool

I'm as attracted to you as a bee to making honey
I'm as attracted to you as children spending money

I'm as attracted to you as my sister to shopping
I'm as attracted to you as a balloon is to popping

I'm as attracted to you as a ship to the sea
I'm as attracted to you as a pod to a pea

I'm as attracted to you as MI5 are to spying
I'm as attracted to you as birds are to flying

I'm as attracted to you as a mop to the floor
I'm as attracted to you as a handle to a door.

**Sophie Wilks (11)**
**Leighfield Primary School, Uppingham**


## Hurricane

I am a hurricane, I can be destructive
And sometimes I can be helpful.
When I am angry, *do not get in my way,*
I lift up houses with people inside and do not care.
When I am tired, I relax in the sun waiting to gather my powers again.

**George Gutteridge (8)**
**Leighfield Primary School, Uppingham**

## A Storm

The storm is an angry sea serpent,
Can be any size,
When you least expect it,
It's right before your eyes.

It's never afraid to attack,
It is big and black,
When you mistake it for a friend,
Your life is going to end.

Then, slowly it crawls away,
Waiting for another day.

**Bethany Turiccki (11)**
Leighfield Primary School, Uppingham


## Mud

Mud on your face,
Mud on your clothes,
Mud on your shirt,
Mud between your toes.

Mud on the floor,
Mud on your knees,
Mud on your socks,
Mud on the cheese.

Mud in the house,
Mud in your shoes,
Mud in your bed,
Mud in the booze.

Mud in your pants,
Mud in your hair,
Mud in the car,
Mud *everywhere!*

**Elliott Bentley (11)**
Leighfield Primary School, Uppingham

## The Rainbow

The rainbow is a fluttering butterfly
Curved and multicoloured
She flies across the sky sometimes
With her graceful spread of colours.

She floats down to the ground
Surrounded by nature, which she calls her home
But she only stays there for a minute or two
To rest upon her throne.

But soon it's time to go
Back across the blue sky
To rest at another place
To be seen back in July.

**Lauren Rootham (11)**
**Leighfield Primary School, Uppingham**


## Mud

Mud in your shoes,
Mud on the floor,
Mud in your sandwiches,
Mud coming through the door.

Mud on your fruit,
Mud at the fair,
Mud in your jumper,
Mud in your hair.

Mud in your socks,
Mud in your bowl,
Mud on your bottom,
Mud mixed with coal.

Mud in your nose,
Mud on the chair,
Mud in your trousers,
Mud everywhere.

**Daniel Pallett (10)**
**Leighfield Primary School, Uppingham**

## White Is The Moon

White is the moon
Shining bright,
Sees a fox
In the twilight night.

Red is the fox
Slim and fast,
Sees a cat
Running past.

Ginger is the cat
Lives left five,
Sees a puffin
In it dives.

Pied is the puffin
Flying by the shore,
Sees an otter
On a slight detour.

Brown is the otter
With gleaming eyes,
Sees a fish
Swimming with the tide.

Multicoloured is the fish,
Sees the moon up high
Round and white
In the night sky.

**Adam MacDonald (11)**
**Leighfield Primary School, Uppingham**

## The Sound Collector
*(Based on 'The Sound Collector' by Roger McGough)*

*'A stranger called this morning
Dressed all in black and grey
Put every sound into a bag
And carried them away'*

The rustling of the paper
The barking of the dog
The crashing of the cutlery
The silence of the fog

The singing of the postman
The chopping of the food
The baaing of the lambs
The girl in a mood

The sliding of the soap
The gushing of the rain
The galloping of the horses
My sister being a pain

The whistling of the kettle
The clucking of the hen
The chirping of the birds
The shouting of the men

The banging of the drum
The ticking of the clock
The engine of the boat
Before it leaves the dock.

**Charlotte Gregg (10)**
**Leighfield Primary School, Uppingham**

## Evil Spell!

Round and round the cauldron go
Around the cauldron and in they go!

A tail of a dog,
An eye of a frog,

A bird's wing,
A bee's sting,

A fang of a bat,
A leg of a cat,

A toe of a pig,
A witch's wig,

A roar of a lion,
A poker-hot iron,

A skeleton's skull,
A head of a bull.

Bubble, bubble, boil and bubble
In the cauldron let's make trouble.

Now we have all the ingredients
This will be a grueling experience.

**Molly King (10)**
Leighfield Primary School, Uppingham


## The Rain

I run down the sky about to have war.
My power is so strong, I can make a flood or capsize a boat.
I like to get people wet, flowers too if they're in my way.
I can be gentle with soft raindrops or more forceful if I get
                                                   angry or upset.

**Josh Christian (9)**
Leighfield Primary School, Uppingham

## Shakespeare's Spell

In our cauldron I do throw
Shredded skin of snake doth go.
Yowl of cat, sombre night,
Hoof of horse, poisoned bite.

Beating heart, owlet's feather,
Withered entrails, change of weather.

Blackened liver, slip of yew,
Jar of moonlight goes in too.

Tooth of rat, fur of bears,
With all this our cauldron flares.

When moonlight shines and thunder drums,
Upon his steed Macbeth doth come.

**Iona Collins (10)**
**Leighfield Primary School, Uppingham**


## The Wind Is A Scatty Wolf

The wind is a scatty wolf,
Cold and strong,
Carrying hats in its teeth
And licking them with his tongue.

But when he starts to howl,
His echoes bark and growl,
He feeds on bones
And groans.

But when the sun is up,
He covers his head with his paws,
He falls asleep and snores,
He calms down,
Just the smallest sound.

**Jennifer Hemmings (10)**
**Leighfield Primary School, Uppingham**

## Witches' Hell Charm

Swooping around the battered bowl,
Striking fear into the hardest soul.
From the pot rises pain,
Then only clouds of death remain.
Despair is the secret key,
Charm a life of horror for thee.

Swirl and swelter, boil and steam,
Macbeth shall utter his final scream.

Blood of baby, tiger relieved of coat,
Tears of crocodile, gizzard of goat.
Skull of koala, maggot in half,
Spine of fish and an evil laugh.
Toe of panther, as dark as night,
Head of cat (it must be white.)
Mix all thorough and all well,
For a most cataclysmic spell.

Swirl and swelter, boil and steam,
Macbeth shall utter his final scream.

Now we add things of darkest magic,
For a curse that shall be tragic.
Soul of prisoner, wallowing in sadness,
Claw of wolf, ripped out in madness.
Lady Death's loving embrace,
Lung of vampire, demon knight's mace.
Belly of dragon and the fire within,
Stink of sewers, pain of pin.

Swirl and swelter, boil and steam,
Macbeth shall utter his final scream.

Filter out all the brittle bone,
Soon Macbeth will be under stone.

**Gregory Sale (11)**
Leighfield Primary School, Uppingham

# The Sound Collector
*(Based on 'The Sound Collector' by Roger McGough)*

*'A stranger called this morning,*
*Dressed all in black and grey,*
*Put all the sounds into a bag*
*And carried them away.'*

The purring of the engine,
The hissing of the snake,
The slamming of the bin,
The cutting of a cake.

The talking of the parrot,
The squelching of the bog,
The crunching of the carrot,
The barking of the dog.

The crackle of the flames,
The ringing of the bell,
The flowing of the Thames,
The echo in the cell.

The singing of the lullaby,
The creaking of the stairs,
The screeching of the crow's cry,
The neighing of the mares.

The ticking of the clock,
The clucking of the chicken,
The clicking of the lock,
The dropping of the pin.

A stranger called this morning,
Life will never be the same,
After she put the sounds into a bag
And just carried them away.

**Beatrix Wignall (11)**
**Leighfield Primary School, Uppingham**

## Attraction

I'm as attracted to you as a dog to a bone
I'm as attracted to you as a boy to a moan
I'm as attracted to you as a mum to a shout
I'm as attracted to you as Victoria to a pout
I'm as attracted to you as a clock to a tick
I'm as attracted to you as a computer mouse to a click
I'm as attracted to you as a poet to write
I'm as attracted to you as a boxer to fight
I'm as attracted to you as a fish to a swim
I'm as attracted to you as a her to a him
I'm as attracted to you as a mother to a child
I'm as attracted to you as the animals to the wild
I'm as attracted to you as a teacher to a frown
I'm as attracted to you as a queen to a crown
I'm as attracted to you as a lady to a necklace
I'm as attracted to you as a hen to a hen house.

**Megan Wright (10)**
**Leighfield Primary School, Uppingham**


## Simile Story Poem

The waves were as tall as mountains.
But the ship was as weak as a twig.
The island was like a spitting fire.
The forest was like an unfriendly giant.
The castle was like a dragon's mouth.
The towers were like crooked teeth.
The guards looked like hungry snakes.
They looked at me as if I was dirt.
I felt as hard as a stone.
I ran like the wind.

**Rosie Mottershead (9)**
**Leighfield Primary School, Uppingham**

## Daddy, While You Were Out

Daddy . . . while you were out a couple of things happened . . .

Someone touched your plasma telly
Your skis got misplaced
Somehow beer bottles got smashed on the carpet
Your watch was dismantled
And the can opener has gone
Your suit's got orange juice on it
The Ferrari hat and jacket somehow ended up in the dog's mouth
Strangely your Valmorel wine was opened
The Blackberry phone has been smashed
Unexplainably someone looked in your folder
Somehow your work phone has deleted everything
And the Top Gear DVD has gone!
Your fuel card has gone
And your driving licence found its way into the scissors
The X-ray of your brain is in the bath and the taps are on
Your walking stick was snapped
Your steel toe-capped boots are somewhere buried in the garden
And Daddy . . . guess what?
Your Ferrari Enzo has vanished
But it wasn't me because
I love your car
Even though I can't go in it.

**Charley Munro Scott (10)**
Leighfield Primary School, Uppingham


## The Wind

The wind is a galloping horse charging its way to glory.
Jumping over high hedges, it tramples bushes as he runs.
Cantering up the long hills that come, it soars past the birds.
Banging through the stable doors, blowing through his puffing nose.
It batters boats while rushing along the seashores.
His cantering gusts blow the people down.
And the sea moans as he rushes by raging along the sandy shore.

**Sabrina Lucas (10)**
Leighfield Primary School, Uppingham

## Witches' Spell

Circle round the cauldron go,
To follow the recipe, pierce a soul.
Slowly add a cry of pain,
Then throw in a lion's mane.
Boil for one cold, murky, full moon,
Then add sweat of a baboon.

The cauldron will steam, boil and bubble,
Fear us Macbeth for this spell's trouble.

Dragon's fire,
Macbeth's desire.
Eagle owl's wing,
Spitting cobra's sting.
Tooth of vampire,
Yellow hammer's choir,
Cool it with unicorn's blood,
Then the charm is firm and good.

The cauldron will steam, boil and bubble,
Fear us Macbeth for this spell's trouble.

Heart ot dog,
Tusk of hog.
Scale of trout,
Brings the charm about.
Maggot's skin,
Guts you must bin.
Liver of piranha,
Tongue of iguana.

The cauldron will steam, boil and bubble,
Fear us Macbeth for this spell's trouble.

Use this charm for whatever reason,
As long as it involves the king's high treason.

**Harry Wade (10)**
**Leighfield Primary School, Uppingham**

## The Sound Collector
*(Based on 'The Sound Collector' by Roger McGough)*

*'A stranger called this morning,*
*Dressed all in black and grey,*
*Put every sound into a bag*
*And carried them away'.*

The cheeping of the robin,
The banging of a door,
The shattering of the glass,
The tapping on the floor.

The barking of the dog,
The creaking of the stairs,
The buzzing of the doorbell,
The sniffing of the hare.

The hissing of a snake,
The ribbiting of a frog,
The laughing of a hyena,
The sawing of a log.

The swaying of a dolphin,
The crashing of the sea,
The bounding of a bunny,
The buzzing of a bee.

The cracking of the ice,
The sizzling of the fire,
The blowing of the wind,
The singing of the choir.

A stranger called this morning,
She didn't leave her name,
Left us only silence,
Life will never be the same.

**Daniel Webster (11)**
**Leighfield Primary School, Uppingham**

## The Night Prowlers

White is the moon
Shining bright
Sees a lion
With some might.

Golden is the lion
Its head held high
Sees a bee
In the sky.

Striped is the bee
Full of glee
Sees a squirrel
Up a tree.

Brown is the squirrel
Full of fun
Sees a leopard
Having a run.

Spotty is the leopard
Having a race
Sees a rabbit
At a pace.

White is the rabbit
Eating some food
Sees a lizard
In a mood.

Green is the lizard
Being so mean
Sees a hamster
Having a clean.

Grey is the hamster
Full of pride
Sees a goldfish
Having a glide.

The sun is up
I have to go
I've seen all animals
High and low.

**Louisa Newell (11)**
Leighfield Primary School, Uppingham

## The Challenge

'I've got a challenge for all of you,
So sit up and listen,' said Mr McHugh.
We waited and waited for him to explain,
Then the blood in my head, it just started to drain.
'Write a *poem!*' he said,
Then my mind went *dead!*
My hand shot up and I told him so,
'I'm not any good at these poems you know.'
I held back my tears and tried not to cry,
And Mr McHugh said, 'Just give it a try!'
I tried to think of a rhyme with thank,
But two hours later my page was still blank.
Words and ideas swirled round in my mind,
As sentences now became harder to find.
I stared at my paper so beautifully white,
Maybe tomorrow I'll know what to write!

**Rebecca Sale (8)**
Leighfield Primary School, Uppingham

## The Pond

I am like glass, my water icy cold.
I am a pond.
Tadpoles have a life with the frogs and grow like the wind.
I've seen circles of love from swans and ducks.
Reeds sway gently giving a bed to the life in me.
I have friends that nobody has ever seen.
My life is cool and calm.

**Angela Wilson (8)**
Leighfield Primary School, Uppingham


## The Sea

I have predators and fish inside me
I can take you under when you're having a dip.
I am kind and angry.
I sink ships, crashing against the rocks.
I am full of salt too.
Sometimes I am quiet and calm.
I hold unknown creatures.
Whirlpools start inside me.

**Thomas Little (8)**
Leighfield Primary School, Uppingham


## Silent Things

Ice glistening in the sun.
The wind whispering.
My tummy grasping for food.
A mouse's tail wiggling.
The breath of a rhino.
A pencil desperate to write.
A wand sleeping in its case.

**Alex Brookes (9)**
Leighfield Primary School, Uppingham

## A Butterfly

I am a butterfly.
I am gentle and fragile.
Fluttering from flower to flower makes me tired.
My enemies are cats and butterfly nets.
I help the flowers grow by collecting pollen.
As I fly by people admire me with my shining colours.
I get angry when I am trapped in hot sweaty hands.
My friends are the worms.

**Phoebe Lawton (9)**
**Leighfield Primary School, Uppingham**


## The Sand

I am the sand brought from the sea,
Soft and smooth and giving fun.
When you play with me,
You make me want to shout out with glee.
But when you play with me out at night,
You make me want to shout with fright.
I feel your soft and smooth hands,
Cuddling me all the time.

**Fay Wilkins (9)**
**Leighfield Primary School, Uppingham**


## Silent Things

The wind whispering.
Coral under the sea.
The breath of a horse.
An apple trapped in a lunch box.
The sand on a beach.
Dust under the carpet.

**Lucy Wade (8)**
**Leighfield Primary School, Uppingham**

## A Rose

My beautiful petals shine in the sun.
I can defend myself with my thorns.
I feel soft like grass, the soft kind.
My perfume is delightful, it makes your nose delight.
I can hurt people by pricking them.
So don't get me *angry!*

**James Aleixo (9)**
Leighfield Primary School, Uppingham


## The Wind

I can be kind and destructive.
But when I'm kind I can carry the scent of a rose.
I can carry a roof off a house.
I can take a flood back into the sea, if I feel generous.
I swirl and dance if I am joyful.

**Alex MacDonald**
Leighfield Primary School, Uppingham


## The Ocean

I crash about like an elephant.
People love to swim in me.
My enemies are fishermen who take my friends away,
That makes me lonely.
At night I am a soft gentle blanket.
I have islands in the middle of me.
I give you fish under the water and coral too.

**Luke Griffiths**
Leighfield Primary School, Uppingham

## Simile Story Poem

The waves were as high as hills.
But the ship was as weak as pencil lead.
The island was like a fiery pit of bones.
The forest was as dark as a cave.
The castle was as tall as Mount Everest.
The towers were like ready spears.
The guards looked as terrifying as hungry wolves.
They looked at me as if I was a puny stick.
I felt as stiff as a statue.
I ran like hunted prey.

**Connor Griggs (9)**
**Leighfield Primary School, Uppingham**


## The Wind

The wind brushes through my hair like a hairdryer.
It helps me to bodyboard on the waves.
My boomerang turns in the wind.
I can be angry and make people cold.
I help the trees and people to breathe.
If I am joyful, I rush around swirling and dancing.
If I am angry, I can lift up houses and cars.

**Harry Stuart (8)**
**Leighfield Primary School, Uppingham**


## Silent Things

The attic sighing.
A spider spinning its web.
The breath of a rhino.
The fire of a barbecue.
The apple trapped in a lunchbox.

**George Newcomb-Harvey (9)**
**Leighfield Primary School, Uppingham**

## The Sea

I can cool you down when you take a dip,
I have no enemies but I eat the sand.
Sometimes I can take down ships
With a little help from my friend, the wind.
I grow all the time and never get smaller.
Treat me nicely, do not pollute me, then I will repay you in kindness.

**Thomas Beach (9)**
Leighfield Primary School, Uppingham


## Tornado Attack!

I can push houses away and lift up rocks.
The ground cracks when it feels my power.
I can swirl people around until they are injured.
When I step on something it makes a big hole.
I punch rooftops off.
However, when I am worn out and finished,
I gather my strength for my return.

**Josh Foley (9)**
Leighfield Primary School, Uppingham


## Oak Tree

I am an old oak tree.
I can be very kind and gentle.
I can give shelter to any living thing.
I give acorns to children when they come by.
I can be thoughtful too.

**Jamie Duggan (9)**
Leighfield Primary School, Uppingham

## Rainbow

A drop of rain, a spot of sun
Put them together, what have you done?
Fiery red is angry and hot
Red is love, red is blood
Orange is juicy, bouncy and bright
Orange is the colour of the setting sun
Yellow is banana and bright
Yellow is the colour of the sun above
Green is peaceful, dark
Green is the colour of big trees
Blue is light and calming
Blue is the colour of the sea
Indigo is sleepy, peaceful and calm
Indigo is the colour of berries
Violet is charming, happy and bright
Violet is the colour of the beautiful flowers.

**Lacey Holbrook (8)**
**Leighfield Primary School, Uppingham**


## Future

I look into the future, what do I see?
A 93-year-old woman staring back at me.

I look in deeper and it's a mirror, oh no!
I am the old lady, I better go.

I feel my chin and my wrinkly skin,
I feel for my hair but it's no longer there.

People talk but I can't even hear,
And I can only see if they're very near.

Oh my gosh, I've grown up fast,
But I suppose life will never last.

**Thea Crutchley (8)**
**Leighfield Primary School, Uppingham**

# Young Writers Information

We hope you have enjoyed reading this book - and that you will continue to enjoy it in the coming years.

If you like reading and writing poetry drop us a line, or give us a call, and we'll send you a free information pack.

Alternatively if you would like to order further copies of this book or any of our other titles, then please give us a call or log onto our website at www.youngwriters.co.uk

**Young Writers Information
Remus House
Coltsfoot Drive
Peterborough
PE2 9JX**

**(01733) 890066**